More books by S.M. LaViolette
& Minerva Spencer:

THE ACADEMY OF LOVE SERIES

THE MUSIC OF LOVE
A FIGURE OF LOVE

THE OUTCASTS SERIES

DANGEROUS
BARBAROUS
SCANDALOUS
NOTORIOUS

THE MASQUERADERS SERIES

THE FOOTMAN

THE SEDUCERS SERIES:

MELISSA AND THE VICAR*
JOSS AND THE COUNTESS*

S.M.'s Historical Erotic Romance Series:
VICTORIAN DECADENCE

HIS HARLOT*
HIS VALET*
HIS COUNTESS*

ANTHOLOGIES:

BACHELORS OF BOND STREET
THE ARRANGEMENT

*Forthcoming

A SECOND CHANCE *For* *Love*

Minerva Spencer

Crooked
Sixpence
CS
P
Press

CROOKED SIXPENCE BOOKS are published by

CROOKED SIXPENCE PRESS
2 State Road 230
El Prado, NM 87529

First printing April 2020

ISBN: 978-1-951662-24-0

10 9 8 7 6 5 4 3 2 1

Any references to historical events, real people, or real places are used fictitiously. Names, characters, and places are products of the author's imagination.

Photo stock by Period Images
Printed in the United States of America.

One

London
1817

J ustin squeezed his eyes shut and rubbed his eyelids—*hard*—
the soft leather of his gloves cool on his hot skin.

But when he opened his eyes, she was still standing
there.

"Well I'll be damned," he murmured. He closed the door to
his carriage with a soft *click* and slumped back against it, unable
to move his gaze from this specter from his past.

Juss was some distance away, and the light was dim, but he
could see her clearly enough, and he'd know that prim mouth,
turned-up nose, and fiery red hair anywhere—although most of
it was covered with a hideous cap right now.

Even though he could see her with his own eyes, he had a
hard time believing it.

She was carrying a large wooden crate down the back steps
of Madam LeMonde's stylish Bond Street dress shop. There was
a small lantern perched on top of the box and it was illuminating
her face in an eerie fashion. Judging by the way she was
staggering, the box was heavy.

A gentleman would help her, his conscience prodded.

But I'm not a gentleman. Juss thought the word with all the loathing he felt for the breed.

He'd known his share of so-called *gentlemen* and a goodly number of them would just as likely push her against the wall and mount her as help her.

So he stayed where he was, his eyes dry from staring—as if she'd disappear if he blinked.

She paused at the bottom of the stairs and lifted one shoulder to rub at something on her jaw, an itch that had inconveniently developed while both her hands were full. The only other light in the narrow mews was from the lamp outside the back entrance of the nearest business, The Greedy Vicar public house.

It had been a decade since he'd last seen her but Justin would have recognized her even if it had been a century: Miss Oona Parker, the woman whose judgmental self-righteousness had sent his life into a downward spiral of poverty and suffering—a spiral that had, at long last, led him here. Miss Oona Parker, his damnation or his salvation, depending on how one looked at things.

She propped the box on her hip and unlocked the heavy wooden door that led to Madam's storage vault. Even from this distance he could see that her movements were slow, almost bone-weary. Well, working as a drudge for a harpy like Madam LeMonde could not be easy. She lifted her burden with both hands and disappeared into the black maw, leaving the door ajar behind her.

Justin turned toward his coachman; Beekman was waiting patiently, wearing his customary bored expression. The two of them had first met in the louse house—not long after he'd seen Miss Parker for the last time—many years before Justin was a wealthy, powerful businessman in a position to offer Beekman—or anyone else—employment. At least not legal employment.

"Return for me in ten minutes" he told Beekman.

"Yes, Mr. Taylor." Beekman clucked his tongue and the four chestnuts leapt forward, quickly disappearing into the velvety darkness of Cork Lane.

Justin didn't normally tool around the city in his traveling coach but he'd just returned from his country house, which was a two hour drive, and he liked to work during the trip rather than take his curricle. Especially when the weather was sharp and chill like it was tonight.

He smelled snow in the air. As if on cue, a large snowflake landed on his nose—a prominent organ that attracted such assaults—and then the sky opened its vaults and the air around him swirled with white fluff that sparkled beneath the lamplight.

Fortunately he had on his heaviest woolen greatcoat even though his plans for the evening had included nothing more adventurous than stopping in at The Greedy Vicar for a meal, a few pints, and the monthly meeting with his manager before going home for the night.

Pure chance had brought him out the back entrance of the pub tonight; otherwise Juss might never have seen her. He usually visited this property just once a month, and almost always in the evening, when most of the other shops in the string of buildings would be closed for the night.

Yes, it had been a night like any other—until now. Until her.

Justin's lips curved into a smile he knew was not nice. What were the bloody odds that he would see her after all these years? Especially *now*?

It had to be fate.

He pulled up his collar and strode through the quickly blanketing snow toward the dark rectangle that led to the building's warren of vaults, his booted heels echoing damply as they struck the cobbles. He paused at the doorway, anticipation causing his pulse to accelerate and sending blood racing through his body. The freezing air chilled the sweat on his brow but he was uncomfortably hot beneath the layers of wool: hot with barely suppressed excitement.

What are you doing, Juss?

Fate has thrown her into my path, it doesn't seem right to ignore this . . . opportunity.

It was a long, long time ago—another life. Leave it be; leave her be.

Juss ignored the voice and peered into the darkness beyond, allowing his eyes to adjust: he'd never listened to his better angel in the past, so why start now?

He knew it would be wiser to take this new information home and think about an approach, but there was no way in hell he was going home without seeing her—talking to her. His mind was blank just now, but he'd know what he wanted to say once he said it. That was his way: quick and confident. That was how he'd grown his measly few pence into shillings and then a handful of pounds, and, finally, into hundreds and thousands of pounds.

On that thought, he headed toward a flicker of light off to the left some fifteen feet ahead. He knew that was where she would be, because that was the storage area reserved for Madam Cecile LeMonde's dress shop. Justin had known Dotty LeMonde since his first year in London, a decade earlier. The woman was from Old Saint Nichols Street and was no more French than he was.

Juss heard Miss Parker before he saw her. There was the sound of something being dragged—a ladder maybe—and the dull clunking of wood on stone.

When he reached the door to the storage area she was at the far side of the large room, perched on a ladder to replace large spools of thread on dowels that had been attached to the low crossbeams.

Justin crossed his arms and leaned against the doorframe to watch her.

He still had no idea what he was going to do—perhaps speak or perhaps just slip away—but he'd do it after she came down off the ladder.

A large, worn overcoat covered her slender body from neck to feet. The only part of her clothing he could see was the high neck of her gown—a serviceable gray—long sleeves, and worn brown ankle boots. She was facing away from him so he studied her shoulders, narrow but straight, her posture so rigid she appeared to have an iron rod in place of a spine.

The stable lads had called her Miss Oona Purity and had taken every opportunity to put themselves in her path. They'd never been openly disrespectful, just teasing and mocking. Of course not far beneath that mockery was desire—at least that's the way it had been for Justin—because she was one of the most beautiful women he'd seen before or since. Small and shapely, with hair like spun copper and big green eyes.

She had ignored them, not even bothering to glance their way most of the time, as if they were the dregs of humanity sprung up from the gutters. Many of them *were* the dregs—including Justin—so it wasn't as if her judging looks were slanderous.

The competition to help her mount and dismount her horse had been fierce but Juss had always made certain that *he* was the one to slide his hands around the beautiful—and haughty—young woman's tiny waist.

Now that Juss was older he realized she must have been rather alone in the viscount's household. Unlike the other servants she ate her meals in her room or sometimes the schoolroom and had very little interaction with the rest of them. She couldn't have been very old—certainly younger than twenty—and the governess position must have been her first.

He'd only spoken to her a few times and she'd kept their conversations brief and to the point, an action that had only made her more unattainable and therefore desirable.

Juss had slept with his first woman at fourteen and they'd not stopped throwing themselves at him ever since. He'd been an arrogant little fuck by the age of twenty-four—which is how old he'd been when he'd met Miss Oona Purity—certain of his ability to charm the birds out of the trees. Or at least to charm one pretty young governess out of her shell.

But she'd barely given him the time of day.

His lips curled up. Well, not until she'd run squealing to the viscount about catching him and Clara.

And here she was in the flesh: Miss Oona Purity.

Juss waited and watched in silence, his mind on the last time he'd seen her—the day his life went to hell.

***

Oona's fingers were so cold they actually *hurt* with it. She'd put on her coat and scarf but, foolishly, hadn't pulled on her gloves. She'd wanted to hurry and finish this before Madam came into the back room after serving her last customer.

The older woman wasn't cruel, but she tended to get short-tempered with her five employees, especially Oona, the only one of the workers who had no skills to offer other than a nimble mind and strong back. She was also the newest employee, having come to Madam just five months ago.

Oona took the last spool from the box and raised it over her head. The dowel was behind her and she'd either have to get down and move the heavy ladder to reach it, or . . . .

It was foolish and dangerous, but she arched her back and stretched, holding the spool over her head. She'd just put the hole near the dowel when her foot slipped a little and sent the rickety ladder wobbling. She shrieked as the spool slipped from her fingers and plummeted to the floor, her body right behind it.

Time stretched and slowed, giving her a moment to imagine how it would feel when she hit the cold stone floor. Oona squeezed her eyes shut, gritted her teeth, and prepared for the worst. And then she slammed into a pair of strong arms, their owner grunting from the force of impact, his knees pressing into her back as he bent to absorb her weight.

The first thing she saw when she opened her eyes was the underside of a masculine, angular jaw. Her rescuer tilted his chin down and eyes like blue flame burned into her as he cradled her body against his broad, unyielding chest.

Oona's brain struggled with the information her eyes provided: high, sharp cheekbones, a firm chin, a prominent Romanesque nose with a bump on the proud curve, and full, sinful lips that were pulled into a mocking smile. His thick, silky black hair was cut into a fashionable crop just long enough to let a lock flop teasingly over his brow.

Her head was warm and muzzy and she felt unnaturally aware of his warm body. No. No, it couldn't be.

"How nice of you to drop in, Miss Parker."

The voice was more polished, but the cockney still lurked beneath the façade.

"Juss." The word was out before she could catch it. Her face heated at the use of his pet name, a privilege he'd never granted her. "Er, Mr. Taylor," she amended.

His mouth pulled up higher on one side, his hooded eyes glinting. "Ah, so you *do* remember me."

As if anyone ever forgot Justin Taylor. Oona could tell by his smug tone that he wasn't surprised at all that she knew who he was.

"Are you hurt?" His low voice vibrated through her body and reminded her she was still tight against his chest.

She squirmed.

7

His arms clenched slightly, as if he might keep her, and her pulse thundered at the thought. But he lowered her with sudden swiftness and her feet hit the ground with a loud clack.

Oona staggered back a step. "Wh-what are you doing here?" she demanded, tilting her head back sharply to meet his gaze; he looked nothing like his former self, and yet he did.

"You're welcome, ma'am." His hat had fallen, likely when he'd caught her, and he bent to pick it up.

Oona's face heated. "Oh. I'm sorry, of course I'm grateful that you were here to catch me. But—"

"In answer to your question, I own this building," he said coolly, but she could hear the pride simmering beneath his words. His full lips were curved into a faint smile, the same smirk he'd always worn in repose. It was remarkable how familiar the expression was even though she'd not seen it for a decade. As ever, he made Oona feel young, ignorant, gauche; that wasn't all he'd made her feel.

But right now it was making her feel like an idiot. "*You're* Mr. Taylor—Mr. Justin Taylor?"

"In the flesh."

"Oh. I never put the two names together," she said, sounding breathy and foolish.

"Taylor is a common name, as is Justin. Why would you ever link your employer's landlord with an impoverished, *disgraced* groom you knew many years ago?"

Oona frowned at the slight but menacing emphasis on the word *disgraced*. Did he think she judged him for losing his position so long ago? The thought made her grimace; if he only knew about how *she'd* lost *her* position. Oona cringed at the thought of the arrogant, confident, and successful man in front of her learning about her mortifying disgrace. And it was clear that he *was* successful. Her eyes flickered over his elegantly clad body: skintight black pantaloons and a wool overcoat that

8

embraced his broad shoulders as closely as a lover, his leather-clad hands holding a high-crowned black beaver hat.

What had happened to him? How had he gone from a groom to . . . *this?* Dozens of questions swirled around in her head like too many fish in a pond. Oona snatched at one, "How long have you known I worked for Madam LeMonde?"

He reached into his pocket and took out his watch. "Perhaps ten minutes."

Why did that make her feel marginally less anxious?

Did you think he was stalking you, Oona?

No, she thought no such thing. In fact, she was more than a little surprised that he would even remember who she was.

He replaced his watch and once again turned his uncomfortable gaze on her.

Oona swallowed, loudly, and his lips twitched: he was enjoying her discomfort.

"Why are you looking at me that way?" she asked.

His eyebrows rose. "What way?"

Oona was good with words, but she had none to describe this particular look.

"I didn't know you were a seamstress as well as a governess," he said when she didn't reply. "But then I suppose that's not surprising as we did not occupy the same spheres—me being in the stables and you being in his lordship's house."

"No, I'm not—" she hesitated, uneasy at what she was about to admit to this man—a man who'd always flustered her, even when he'd been a mere groom. And now. . .

"Yes?" he prodded. "You're not . . ."

"I'm not a seamstress; I'm the all-around dogsbody." She'd not meant to sound so belligerent, but there it was.

"You didn't like governessing?"

"Yes, actually, I enjoyed it a great deal."

"Ah, I see."

Oona was about to ask him just what it was he saw, but then she wasn't sure she wanted to hear the answer.

He glanced around and then stooped to pick up the spool. "Where does it go?"

"Oh, you don't have to—"

He sighed.

"Fine." She pointed to the second to last dowel. "By the navy thread."

He had to stand on his toes to slide it onto its holder, but it was done in a blink.

"Are you finished here?" he asked.

"Yes. I just need—" but he'd already bent to pick up her empty box and lamp.

"Come, I'll walk you out." His tone was peremptory—commanding. Certainly not the tone a groom would use. But then he wasn't a groom anymore, was he?

When he opened the door, Oona gasped. "Oh, how lovely." She stared up at the dark sky, the view a dizzying one as thousands of glinting flakes hurtled toward her.

When he said nothing she turned to find him staring at her from beneath heavy lids. "Yes, isn't it?" he said, and then pulled the door shut with a sharp snap, his eyes never leaving hers.

"Um." Oona reached a shaking hand into her coat pocket for the heavy key. "I need to—"

He held up a ring with a half-dozen keys. "I've already locked it."

"Do you always—"

"Finish other people's sentences?" His lips curved that same non-smile. "No, not always." He gestured toward Cork Street, where she saw a luxurious black coach with four restless chestnuts. "May I offer you a ride anywhere, Miss Parker—*is* it still Miss Parker?"

"No—I mean, yes." She shook her head at her bumbling. "Yes, it's still Miss Parker. No, I don't need a ride as I've not finished work for the evening." She remembered her manners at the last moment. "But thank you."

He handed her the box and lamp and then bowed. "I wish you a good evening, Miss Parker."

Like a street urchin staring in a shop window, Oona watched as he made his way to the magnificent carriage, his booted feet muffled by the thin layer of snow. He opened the door and hopped in without steps, his greatcoat fluttering like a dark flag in the snow-dotted night.

Oona wondered if he'd look back before he closed his door.

But he didn't and the carriage rolled away into the darkness.

Two

The beautiful, fluffy white snow from the night before had turned into a brownish-gray sludge that stained a good four inches of Oona's hem. Fortunately she'd worn her oldest woolen gown, a tobacco-shade that had once been rich with golden undertones but was now the color of dirt. Or mud, would be more appropriate.

It took forty-five minutes to walk to Madam LeMonde's but Oona had more time for walking than she had money for a hackney. Besides, she liked walking, even when the weather was cold and the streets filthy; it gave her time to think. She'd thought working as a dogsbody would give her time to think, but her mind merely focused on the tasks at hand during a day filled with tedious minutia and manual labor. It was nothing like teaching; when she taught, her thoughts had been as rich as a tapestry.

Spilt milk.

Indeed, she thought as she gave a farthing to the young boy who risked life and limb to sweep a path across the busy street. Yearning for the days when she'd been a governess was pointless. Oona usually did a good job of forgetting, but seeing Juss Taylor—*Mr. Taylor to you*—brought it all back with a painful ache.

Oona shivered and pulled her old gray coat tighter around her as she scurried through the early morning light, her mind returning yet again to last night—to Juss and the feel of his powerful arms around her body.

"Not today," Oona said with regret as she hurried past a young girl holding a basket of oranges. She had no extra money—not even for an orange—and needed every penny to purchase a seat on the stage out of London in six days. She knew she should probably wait until she'd saved more money, but if she didn't visit Katie now, it would be months before she'd have another two days off together, which is what she needed as it took half a day just to get to Katie's school.

Madame LeMonde's shop was sandwiched between the Greedy Vicar pub and Hungry Mind bookstore. The bookstore wasn't open this early but Gabriel St. Aulyn, the handsome proprietor gave her a friendly wave as he unlocked the door to his shop.

Oona had to step around a huge wagon full of casks and crates already filling the mews behind the pub.

"Good morning, Miss Parker," the manager of the Greedy Vicar called out.

"Good morning, Mr. Shaw," Oona replied, oddly warmed by the friendly, but polite, acceptance of the two men.

Just as she was heading for the steps to LeMonde's the owner of Bond Street Coffee & Tobacco, Mr. Gaines, passed through the mews on his way to the storage vaults.

Mr. Gaines tipped his high crowned beaver at Oona and nodded at Mr. Shaw. "Good morning to you both," he said with a pleasant, if somewhat distracted smile—the look of a man with a long list of tasks on his mind.

Mr. Gaines was a very attractive Black man who'd only recently opened his shop. He moved with the efficient decisiveness of someone determined to see that his new business flourished.

Oona had gone to the coffee and tobacco shop's grand opening and had enjoyed both the delicious coffee and pastries. Mr. Gaines had shown that, in addition to being a business man, he was also kind, and had offered the employees who worked near the coffee shop a substantial discount on any pastries which had not sold by the end of the business day. Already his generosity had meant Oona didn't need to eat porridge every night of the week.

Oona began unwinding her muffler as she climbed the back steps to the dress shop. Looking at the entrance to the vault made her stomach tighten as she recalled last night—not that she needed the sight of the building to remind her of the odd encounter with Mr. Justin Taylor, an encounter she'd been relentlessly reliving all night long.

Oona grimaced at her racing thoughts, for once grateful for the mindlessness of her work; it would be a relief to have a few hours not thinking about him.

She closed the door to the shop and hung her muffler on the hook that was reserved for her. She'd just taken the pin from her hat when the door to the small office where Madam kept her books flew open and bounced against the wall, making her jump.

"Good morning, Madam Le—"

"You ungrateful wretch," the older woman thundered, her French accent sloughing away like skin from a snake.

"Wha—"

"Don't act like you don't know what's goin' on," she snapped in cold, hard Cockney. "It'll just make things worse for you."

"But—"

"You should have waited until somebody *else* used the key to the vault—that would have been wiser."

"The vault?"

Maria, Madam's assistant clerk, came from the front of the shop, her face a mask of mortification as she looked at Oona. "Perhaps you might let her explain, Madam?" she asked faintly.

LeMonde didn't take her eyes off Oona. "What's there to explain? She is a thief. I've already sent Will to fetch the constable; he'll be back any moment."

Oona felt as if she'd drifted off to sleep and fallen face first into a nightmare. "I stole nothing from you." Oona shook her head, although the other woman hadn't spoken. "It's unjust of you to assum—"

"You have the key."

Oona blinked. "No, I'm sure I—" Then suddenly she recalled who'd locked the door last night: it had been Mr. Taylor. She dug through the pockets of her coat, even though she knew they contained nothing but her gloves and handkerchief because she'd had her hands in her pockets all the way to work. She tore open her reticule and dumped the contents on the nearby work table: a few coins, a card of pins, a frazzled silk flower that she'd found in the park on her walk, and the small leather case that held her miniature of Katie.

And the heavy iron key to the vault.

"A-ha!" LeMonde snatched the key off the table as if Oona might take it.

"I'm sorry, I forgot—I—" Oona stopped. What could she possibly say?

I was overcome after just being rescued by the most distracting man I've ever met and so I must have dropped the key into my reticule rather than put it back in its place. . . .

It was the truth, but it was hardly one Oona wanted to share—nor did she think the other woman would believe her.

"But, Madam, why would she bring the key with her if she was the thief?" Marie asked, risking LeMonde's wrath for

Oona—an action Oona never would have expected from the other girl.

Madam snorted. "How do I know what a thief thinks? No doubt she hoped to replace it and none would be the wiser." She crossed her arms over her ample bosom and leaned against the door, as if Oona might make a break for it.

Oona met Maria's eyes and the other woman gave a slight shrug, as if to say she had done all she could.

"Won't you give me a chance to explain myself?" Oona asked.

"You can explain it to the constable."

"But Madam, I don't—"

The older woman's eyes flickered to something over Oona's shoulders, and her entire demeanor transformed from a vengeful harpy to a pliable, voluptuous siren. Oona knew who'd walked in the door before Madam LeMonde even spoke.

"Thank God, you're here, Juss. You're just in time to help me deal with this."

Oona gritted her teeth at the woman's casual, almost sensual, use of his pet name; this would not end well for her. She sighed and turned.

In the light of day she could see the subtle signs of age she'd not noticed last night in the near darkness. Crow's feet at the corners of his eyes, a deep, crescent-shaped groove on the right side of his mouth, likely the result of all the smirking he did, and even a few flecks of gray in his inky black hair. He was dressed for riding and looked twice as broad and even taller in his caped coat and glossy black top boots. He took off his hat and held it under one arm, his unearthly blue eyes moving from Madam LeMonde to Maria before settling on Oona. "What seems to be the problem, Miss Parker?"

Madam LeMonde gave an outraged squeak. "Why are you asking *her*—"

He raised his hand, the one still holding the crop, in a staying gesture. "One at a time, please."

To Oona's amazement, the other woman remained silent, if seething.

"Miss Parker," he prodded.

"She accused me of stealing."

His eyebrows rose slightly and he turned to the dressmaker. "What do you think she stole from you?"

"There are all kinds of things missing from the vault—two bolts of silk, a package of ostrich feathers, a cask of paste jewels for slippers." She cut Oona a slit-eyed look. "I might not have noticed for days had the door not been flapping open when I arrived this morning."

"The door was open?" he said sharply.

"You should tell the other tenants to check their vaults because she might have stolen more."

Mr. Taylor's gaze was heavy on Oona while the other woman spoke. "How long were you here after I saw you in the—"

"You *saw* her last night?" LeMonde shrieked.

He grimaced. "I'm right *here*, Dotty. You needn't yell."

Oona wasn't surprised the modiste's name was Dotty rather than Celine, but she was surprised that Juss Taylor knew and used it.

"What time, Miss Parker?"

Oona forced herself to focus on the moment, rather than this man's possible relationship to her employer. "I left perhaps five minutes after you. When I came back up to the shop Madam had already locked the front door and was ready to go." She shrugged. "I took off my apron, found my gloves, and left."

"Is that true?" he asked LeMonde.

She nodded grudgingly.

"And then you took a hackney home?" he asked.

Oona shook her head. "No, I walked."

"You *walked* home in a blizzard? In the dark?"

Oona was hardly going to tell *this* man that she couldn't afford to pay for a hackney. "What of it? I like the snow."

"It means nothing that she walked," LeMonde said. "She had the key *with* her. She must 'av—*have*—come back with a carriage—and likely an accomplice or two."

"You had the key?" he asked.

Oona's face heated. "Yes, I—I forgot to return it last night."

The faint smile on his full lips told her he knew exactly why she forgot: because she was flustered. Because of him.

"Did you come back later on and steal from Madam LeMonde's vault?" he asked her.

"Of course not," Oona snapped.

He turned to the modiste. "There you have it, Dotty: Miss Parker is not your thief."

Madam LeMonde made a sound like an enraged goose. "You're just going to take 'er *word* for it?"

"Have no fear, I shall get to the bottom of this," he assured her, a chill in his voice and a dangerous glint in his eyes. "I dislike thievery on any of my properties. In the meantime, draw up a list of what is missing and I will see that you are reimbursed. After all, I am responsible for the safety of goods kept on my property."

Madam LeMonde's impressive bosom was rising and falling faster than ever. "And what about *her*?"

"Does she still have her position here?" he asked.

LeMonde snorted.

"Well, then it is none of your concern, is it?"

LeMonde's lips parted, but no words came out.

Justin Taylor fixed his uncomfortably piercing gaze on Oona and said in a silky voice. "I shall see to Miss Parker."

Three

They said nothing to each other as Justin Taylor led her from the dress shop.

Outside there was a young boy walking a magnificent black horse up and down the mews, steam billowing from the mouths of both horse and boy.

"I'll hold Brummel," Mr. Taylor said when the boy stopped in front of them. "Go fetch a hackney and bring it back here. I'll send a man back to fetch the horse."

"Aww, guv! I can bring 'im to yer ken."

The two males locked eyes and some form of wordless communication passed between them before Taylor nodded and then handed him the reins.

The boy grinned wide enough to split his face. "I'll 'av an 'ack in a twinkle, Mr. Juss." He turned tail and scampered off, the horse prancing cooperatively beside him.

Oona looked up at him. "An employee of yours?"

He tapped his whip against his boot as he looked down at her, pausing before answering, another annoying habit of his she'd recalled last night. It was a lazy pause, as if he wasn't quite sure he could be bothered to speak the words. "Never seen him before."

"And you just gave him your horse?"

He nodded slowly. "Mmm-hmm."

"But he knew your name."

"Yes, he knows who I am." The inference was clear: lots of people knew who he was, and those who did would not steal from him.

He wasn't frowning or scowling or speaking in a threatening tone, he simply dripped danger. Oona didn't like her body's response—what sort of woman found danger . . . arousing? Of course her body had always reacted oddly to this man, although it seemed she had even a more severe case of whatever it was now than she'd had then.

She swallowed and looked up; yes, he was still staring. Her mouth opened and words came out, "Brummel is an unusual name for a horse."

"Is it?" he asked with a smirk.

Oona knew that was all he would say unless she asked. "Why would you name your horse after Mr. Beau Brummel?"

She saw a gleam of humor in his eyes. "He's vain and impeccably turned out, it seemed to fit."

Before she could come up with a suitable answer a hackney rolled down Cork Street. When it stopped Mr. Taylor handed her inside and then said something to the driver before climbing in and taking the seat across from her.

"Where are you taking me?" Oona asked when he seemed content to sit in silence while she had suddenly begun to shake, a delayed reaction to being accused of thievery and almost thrown into gaol.

"Home."

"You—you know where I live?"

"No. I thought we'd just drive around a while—perhaps get lucky and find it."

A slightly hysterical laugh broke out of her at his sarcastic response and Oona clasped her hands together to keep them from shaking. "Why are you doing all this, Mr. Taylor?"

"Call me Juss. Or Justin, if you must," he said, turning back to the window.

"Why did you help me, *Juss*?"

"Because I know you didn't steal anything from that vault."

Oona ignored the thrill of joy that seized her at his words. "How do you know that?"

"I just do." He sounded bored, as if her questions were something that had to be tolerated, like bad weather.

What a maddening, obnoxious, high-handed man.

Oona took a deep breath and suppressed her annoyance; he was also the man who'd just liberated her from the bowels of hell. "I appreciate your faith in me, but—"

"Why were you working as a drudge for LeMonde?"

"That's hardly your affair, is it?" she snapped.

Rather than be insulted by her rudeness, he laughed.

Oona bit her lip. "I'm sorry, I shouldn't have said that."

"You can say whatever you like."

"I *know* I can say whatever I like, but that doesn't mean you deserve my churlish behavior. I'm sorry."

He shrugged.

"Why did you involve yourself this morning?"

"Why not?"

Oona returned her teeth to her lower lip to keep from saying something she would immediately regret. She'd never met a more unresponsive man in her entire life. He gave away *nothing*, his face a harsh, unreadable mask.

"Why aren't you working as a governess?"

"That is also none of your affair."

"What are you going to do now?" he asked, undeterred, his gaze lazy as he stared through the dim light of the carriage, as if he didn't care one way or another *what* happened to her.

Oona briefly closed her eyes. God. What *was* she going to do? She'd sold the last four pearls to pay for Katie's most recent semester, but that would be over soon. And here she was with no job and nothing else to sell.

Oona opened her eyes to find he was still staring. "To answer your question, I don't know what I'm going to do. I'll look for something else, I suppose."

"I doubt LeMonde will give you a recommendation," he said.

"I'm accustomed to finding work without a decent recommendation."

"Why is that, Miss Parker? What happened to you? Why are you no longer a governess?"

"Because I have no references," she said, maddened by shame into answering him. "And no one would employ a woman my age without them. There," she spat the word at him. "Are you satisfied now?"

"Why don't you have any references?"

Oona suppressed a growl of frustration. "Because I am a governess who aimed too high, *Mister* Taylor."

His hooded eyes opened wider, his expression one of disbelief. Why was that somehow more insulting than him believing that she was a light-skirt? Oona refused to look away from him even though her face and head were so hot they felt close to exploding. What an insulting, obnoxious, irritating—

"I have a position available."

She gave a rude snort of disbelief. "*You* have a job for *me*?"

His lips curved into that wicked smile that made her entire body throb. "Yes."

"Why would you help me find a new position? We knew each other for a short time a long time ago," Oona narrowed her eyes at him. "I'm stunned you even recognized me as you always seemed far too busy with all your—" She stopped, mortified by what she'd been about to say.

He cocked his head. "I'm so flattered you noticed my activities. Don't stop now—I was busy with all my . . . ?"

Oona's head became so hot it was a wonder she didn't burst into flames and set the carriage on fire.

Well, the damage was already done; she might as well finish the job. "You can mock," she said. "But you know what I mean. None of the servants at the viscount's house ever liked me and you were most certainly their ringleader." His eyebrows rose and Oona stopped. What was *wrong* with her? He'd saved her from going to gaol. Why was she being so combative?

"I apologize for my outburst." Oona forced the words through gritted teeth. "I should be thanking you, not accusing you."

He chuckled and the sound slithered around her body like a snake. "Don't thank me yet. You don't know what the position is."

"I'm s-sorry?"

"You heard me."

Oona stared at him and he stared back. She opened her mouth to ask, but couldn't seem to manage the words. His relaxed posture told her that he was contented to watch her in silence; the only way he'd give her any further information was if she scraped up the courage to ask.

So she swallowed convulsively and then said, "W-what kind of position?"

The right side of his mouth pulled up slowly. "The position of mistress—*my* mistress."

Four

The expression of shock and horror and disbelief on her face was amusing, even if it wasn't very flattering toward Juss. Of course her body language said something else entirely. He'd seen the same reaction in women times beyond counting. Not women of his class, but women of hers. Gentlewomen who were both attracted and repelled by his physicality; women who saw him as a 'bit of rough,' a prospect they found physically—if not mentally—arousing.

Justin let her squirm just a moment longer before saying, "Don't worry, Miss Parker, I don't mean you'd *really* need to become my mistress, I just need you to assume the title for a week."

Juss wondered if it was possible for a human jaw to come unhinged and had just begun to think she'd never speak to him again—about *anything*—when she said, "How much?"

"I beg your pardon?" he asked, even though he knew exactly what she meant. He just wanted to hear her say it again.

"How much will you pay me and for how long?" The words had icicles on them.

"Seven hundred pounds for seven days."

Her gasp cut through the cold air of the carriage. "A hundred pounds a day," she whispered hoarsely.

Juss didn't think it was a question so he didn't answer. Instead he watched her from beneath lowered lids, amused that she didn't seem to notice or care that she was showing her hand so clearly. Oh yes, she would take this position, there was no doubt about it.

Her lips were parted and her eyes were wide, her breathing shallow and rapid. Juss knew he should feel bad about the offer because he was positive she couldn't afford to refuse it. The truth was that as amusing as it would be to have her company, he didn't really need her to make the venture—one he'd been contemplating for a full decade—fulfilling. But providence, it seemed, had dropped her into his lap. Who was he to reject such a gift?

Besides, the trip North was long and tedious and he'd enjoy toying with that prim reserve of hers and seeing what was beneath it. He'd also enjoy learning just how she'd fallen off her pedestal of virtue.

In sum, he'd enjoy having her company for a week.

"Seven hundred pounds for seven days," she said again, as if the words were some kind of talisman. She cut him a nervous glance. "And you say I just need to assume the *title* of mistress?" Her eyes flickered over his person in a way that made his breath catch. His cock was certainly interested in her, but the notion of paying any woman for sexual favors—and that included whores—was repugnant to him.

If Juss wanted her, she'd come to him freely.

"I'll secure adjoining rooms at the posting inns and we'll certainly have our own rooms at the house where we'll be staying. So, no," he gave her a half-smile, "warming my bed is not part of your mistressly duty."

He saw relief on her heart-shaped face, but there was something else, too—regret? Or was that merely arrogant, wishful thinking? Likely the latter.

"I don't understand," she said. "Why would you need me to pretend to be your mistress? Surely you can secure a real one?"

He smiled. "That is none of your affair, Miss Parker."

Her eyes narrowed at his words, which echoed hers, and he knew she wanted to give him a blistering set-down. But she wanted the money more. "Starting when?"

"I'm leaving the day after tomorrow."

"But—but—"

"You sound like a hen, Miss Parker."

Her green eyes, which made emeralds appear dull by comparison, widened and she opened her mouth—no doubt to scold or snap at him—but then she closed it, her forehead furrowing.

"Go on," he said. "Ask everything you can think of right now."

"That doesn't give me much time—not even a week to change my. . . well, not much time."

She swallowed, her expression almost tragic. In Justin's experience only one thing made a woman look so forlorn: a lover.

"Did you have plans next week, Miss Parker?"

She took a deep breath and then let it out slowly. "Nothing that can't be changed."

Juss's curiosity was roused more than was good for him—or the woman across from him.

He'd just decided to give it free rein when she said, "My clothing." She gestured to her person, as if Juss might not know what clothing was. "I'm not prepared for a country hou—"

"I'll pay for clothing appropriate for my mistress."

"Appropriate clothing," she repeated the words carefully, her cheeks flushing darkly.

Juss wanted to laugh; just what the hell was she imagining in that beautiful head of hers? Clearly something scandalous—as if he were planning to dress her in a fig leaf, or less.

"Yes, appropriate," he confirmed in a deliberately silky tone. "I will purchase clothing for your body that pleases me." She jolted at the word *body* and it was all he could do not to laugh. Whatever act of debauchery she'd engaged in to lose her governessing job, it must have been on the tame side if the mere discussion of garments could make her so anxious. Juss smiled; this was a perk he'd not expected.

You're a bad, bad man, Justin Taylor.

Oh yes, he was. But then he'd always known that. Miss Parker had probably suspected he was bad all along, and now she knew for certain.

"How will you find clothing in such a short time?" she asked.

"If you agree to my offer we will turn around and go shopping right now."

She licked her lips, the unintentionally sensual gesture causing him to stiffen. "I assume you need an answer quickly?"

He smiled.

"Very well, I accept." She said the words so swiftly they all ran together. "But I shall want half the money in advance."

Juss could hold his laughter in check no longer: this was going to be the best damned country house party he'd ever attended.

Five

By the time Juss brought her back to the hovel where she lived it was after dark. He'd sent a message home from the modiste shop where he'd taken her, and his carriage had come to fetch them.

The carriage was full of boxes and packages—clothing she would need for the journey— but the bulk of the new clothing would be delivered by the end of the day tomorrow and transported to the house party in the traveling coach that held his valet and the maid he'd engaged for her.

"Give Charles your key and he will take up your packages," Juss told her as they stood under the lamp glow cast by his carriage. She frowned, likely irked by his peremptory tone, but took the key from her reticule and handed it to the footman.

It had begun to snow again around three o'clock and the temperature had turned bitingly cold as the sun went down. Juss was glad he'd insisted on purchasing the big fur muffler and fur-lined cloak she was now wearing.

He waited until Charles disappeared inside the building before looking down at her. "I won't see you again until I come to collect you in two days." He could tell by her widening eyes that his words surprised—and probably pleased—her. "I want you to have tomorrow to reconsider your decision," he said, not stopping when he heard her soft gasp. "If you are not here when I come for you, I will know your answer."

Her lovely lips parted, but words seemed to be eluding her. Well, he was no less stunned by his offer. But several hours spent watching her today had given him qualms. Although she'd as good as claimed to be a fallen woman, she behaved with a dignity and modesty that told him she'd not fallen very far. While taking her on this journey would not hurt her—at least not physically—it would most certainly mortify her sensibilities. So, he'd give her this last chance.

Feeling a bit guilty, are you? The taunting voice in his head prodded. *Because you're all but pushing her away, old chap.*

Was he feeling guilty about bringing her along under a false—or at least unstated—pretext?

The question made him uncomfortable—itself an unusual reaction for a man who never let any finer feelings concern him. Yes, she'd been the cause of his dismissal all those years ago, but did she really deserve what he had planned for her: embarrassment at best and humiliation at worst?

"But—all this," she said, gesturing to her new apparel, and scattering his thoughts. "Won't you—"

Juss gave an irritable shrug. "Keep it. What the devil would I do with it? Whatever you decide, it is yours," he said shortly, suddenly so bloody tired he could hardly stand upright.

That would be your guilt talking, mate.

"But you spent—"

"That isn't your concern," he snapped, distracted by the annoying voice in his head, the way her teeth caught her pillowy lower lip, and the dark flush on her pale-as-snow cheeks.

"What about the m-money?"

Ah, the money. Her question—and the slight stutter over the word *money*—made him smile. It also made him respect her even more than he already did: she was willing to demand what she wanted, even when her bargaining position was less than powerful. He had stopped at his bank before commencing their orgy of shopping, procuring a bearer banknote for the entire amount—an action which had rendered her speechless.

"If you change your mind I trust you will dispose of the note, Miss Parker."

She opened her mouth, but before she could speak the footman stepped out of her building. Good, Juss hardly wished to stand here and persuade her to come on a journey that would only end in embarrassment—even if it would earn her enough money to live for several years.

"Charles will see you to your door," he said, giving her a brief bow before climbing back into the carriage and shutting the door, suddenly eager to put distance between them.

Juss didn't want to, but he turned to look out the window— just one last look. Their eyes met, and then she turned and walked away.

Six

The twenty-four hours that followed the shopping expedition were both the longest and shortest of Oona's life and she was grateful that she could spend them alone. Without her job at Madam LeMonde's to occupy her she had nothing but time.

The first thing she did was write two messages: one to Katie to tell her she wasn't coming, and one to Mrs. Landers, the headmistress at the small school, to say that her plans had changed and request that she keep Katie over this coming weekend. Oona wouldn't send the letters until tomorrow. If she decided not to go, then she could tear up the letters and nobody would be the wiser.

But then there was the issue of the clothing; Oona couldn't keep such expensive items if she didn't accept his offer. One way or another, she would make sure he received all the garments back if she changed her mind. The fur cloak alone was worth more than she made in five years, so he could either sell them or give them to his next mistress or set fire to them. But the one thing he could not do was force her to keep them.

Not that she didn't covet them with a ferocity that left her weak and dizzy. Oona had never thought of herself as a materialistic woman—at least not for anything but books, which she treasured above all other possessions—but these clothes certainly brought out the covetousness in her.

As soon as he'd dropped her at home she laid everything out on her small pallet bed. It was good to have them out in the open—to remind her of what she would be giving away if she changed her mind. Oh, not just the clothing, but all the money that went along with it.

By eight o'clock she was so exhausted from thinking about the matter she put on every stitch of clothing she owned—not the new clothing, which lay on her bed as if they were honored guests—and slept wrapped in her blanket in front of her tiny cookstove.

By midnight there was a thick layer of ice on her water basin. By two in the morning she'd fed the last of her coals into the fire. By three o'clock it was so cold that her fingers were blue and she broke down and donned the beautiful fur-lined gloves before burrowing beneath the heavy fur cloak, taking care not to soil or damage either.

The weather barely warmed with the rising sun and Oona knew she'd need to use some of her dwindling 'emergency' money to buy more coal.

Seven nights for seven hundred pounds—that would be enough money to last for years.

Those were the words that marched relentlessly through her head after she carefully removed all her finery and extra clothing and then shrugged into her old, tattered coat, hat, and mittens, and set out on her errand.

Her eyes watered from the cold, the tears freezing on her lashes, as she walked beneath the iron gray sky, her empty coal scuttle banging against her leg with each step.

As cold as it was, the walk was good for her. Sitting at home in the tiny, freezing, dingy flat only made her mind spin faster. She could have asked the landlady to send up coal but the cost was almost double that of the old man who sold it from his wheelbarrow at the end of Petticoat Alley.

Seven nights for Katie's security, she thought as she handed over the small scuttle along with a sizeable portion of her coins.

More people were already up and about on the journey back to her flat; it was a working day in her neighborhood—for everyone but Oona.

Seven nights would secure a small cottage somewhere far away from dirty, dangerous, brutal London.

Back in her lodgings Oona fed the hungry stove and set about preparing her usual breakfast.

Today was day three on her tea leaves, an economy measure she'd practiced ever since moving to London, but when she looked at yesterday's limp, frozen leaves in the bottom of her pot she decided to splurge. Why not? Tomorrow would have been shopping day—if she'd not lost her job—and there was barely enough tea left to brew a pot. Live for today.

Fifteen minutes later, armed with tea and dry toast, she bundled up and sat in front of her pallet, staring at the beautiful garments while she warmed her hands around her chipped teacup.

In addition to the beautiful fur-lined cloak, muffler, and gorgeous black felt and fur hat, there were two traveling costumes, two nightgowns, and numerous underthings. Most important were the brand new black ankle boots that sat swathed in tissue inside their own box.

Oona looked down at her own battered footwear, which she'd repaired so often they looked like shoes made from patches. Her eyes drifted back to the shiny new ankle boots and she groaned. It was all so beautiful. But was that all it took to purchase her? Some beautiful garments?

And seven hundred pounds—which means when you are finished with this week you can go to Katie and stay with her. You'll be able to be with her at Christmas for the first time in three years.

Yes, all of that was true.

And of course you'll also get seven nights with him, the small voice added gleefully.

The teacup shook badly in her hands. All night long she'd tried to ignore the heavy throbbing that pulsed between her thighs at the mere thought of spending seven days with him. She'd hoped it would be easier to manage her desires in the cold light of day, but it turned out she burned for him no matter what time of day or night. The sorry truth was that the thought of seven days and nights with him was every bit as enticing as the money and beautiful clothing.

Oona had forgotten many things in the almost three decades she'd been alive, but one of the things she'd *not* forgotten was the sight of Justin Taylor's mostly nude, muscular body thrusting into one of the female servants who'd swarmed him like bees to a hive.

She'd meant what she'd said in the carriage—none of the viscount's servants had liked her. It hadn't been just their natural suspicion of a governess—a woman who was neither fish nor fowl—it had been Oona in particular.

Most of their standoffishness, she now knew, had been her fault. She'd just turned seventeen and had been concerned about establishing her authority in the viscount's household so she'd assumed haughty, cool manners that were not her own. Rather than gaining her respect, her behavior had made her unpopular.

Juss, on the other hand, had easily been the most popular of the thirty or so servants; men respected him and women adored him, and he seemed to fit in wherever he was. Even the viscount's haughty butler had deferred to him, although he'd been a mere groom.

Of course Juss Taylor could never be a *mere* anything.

He'd looked as comfortable in the modiste shop today—this one owned by a *real* Frenchwoman—as he'd always been in the masculine confines of the stables.

Madam Thérèse and her clerks had fluttered around him like a host of butterflies around a particularly tasty flower. He'd lounged in the big armchair, which the wily dressmaker kept especially for her male guests, his big body clothed as elegantly as any peer's.

Not that you would mistake him for a member of the aristocracy. Not only was he too big—too muscular and powerfully built—but he brimmed with an energy that was the antithesis of the languid aristocrat. Even before he opened those full, sensual lips and spoke in that oddly rough accent a person knew there was nothing effete about Justin Taylor.

Oona poured the last of the tea from the pot, her mind going back to the day she'd stumbled upon Juss and his mystery lover. She'd been a maiden, an innocent seventeen year-old who'd had no idea what her body's fierce reaction had meant. The night after she'd seen them in the linen closet she had touched herself for the first time, the result both explosive and mortifying and, ultimately, something she wanted more of. So when Edward came to her bedroom not long after Juss had been discharged Oona had allowed him in. It had been madness to believe what he'd told her: that he'd grown to love her and would marry her once his mourning period was finished. But she'd been so lonely and young and he'd been handsome and so very persuasive.

Over the years she'd wondered what Edward would have done if she'd turned him away? Although his approach had been light and lover-like, she now suspected she would have been looking for a new position sooner rather than later if she'd denied him entry to her bed.

As usual, thinking about Edward left her feeling gnawed on and hollow.

So Oona pushed Viscount Venable from her mind. Instead, she turned her attention to the beautiful garments that lay on the bed, and to the man who'd bought them for her.

Seven

Justin didn't know whether Oona Parker would be waiting for him, or not. He also didn't know whether he wanted her to be there, or not. His anger at her—an anger that had simmered for almost a decade—had cooled over the past twenty-four hours.

What about Clara? the implacable voice of vengeance demanded.

Clara would have been discharged whether or not Oona Parker said a word, and Juss knew that for a fact. No matter how much he wanted to blame her, it wasn't Oona's fault Clara had died in childbed in a St. Giles hovel while Justin was picking oakum to pay for his stupidity.

It was Venable's fault, not Oona's, not Clara's, and not even Justin's.

When the carriage stopped Juss opened the door without waiting for Charles, his footman.

"I'll go up," he said, already on his way.

"Very good, sir."

Juss climbed the stairs to the top floor of the dilapidated building two at a time, eager to end this, one way or another.

As to what he'd feel if she wasn't on the other side of this door? Juss sighed; he'd already chased these thoughts around in his head for far too many hours. He was bloody exhausted by the subject.

He raised his hand to knock but the door opened before his knuckles made contact with the wood. Juss gaped. He'd selected her clothing from Madam Thérèse's small collection of ready-made garments, but he'd not seen her in anything except her coat and cloak. The visit to the modiste had been traumatic enough for her; he'd not wanted to humiliate her by making her model for him while the curious eyes of the dressmaker looked on.

He'd known the green wool of her traveling costume—a shade or two darker than her eyes—would look well with her fiery hair, and he'd been correct. She was a small woman but curvy and soft in all the right places. At just a touch over six feet Juss towered over her. He reckoned she couldn't be too much over five feet.

"You look lovely," he hesitated and then added, "Oona."

She startled at the sound of her name and Juss thought she was on the verge of chastising him for such a liberty but must have recalled she was supposed to be his mistress.

"Thank you," she said, swallowing hard and drawing his eyes to the high neck of her spencer and the delicate white skin of her throat. Something about the prim and proper sight made his mouth fill with moisture. She'd been lovely dressed in rags; she was breathtaking with clothing that fit and flattered her.

"I'll g-get my cloak."

Juss followed her into the dismal but impeccably clean room she called home. On the narrow pallet bed were two bags, her cloak, and the ridiculous fur muffler. The rest of the room was bare, as if nobody lived in it.

They both reached for the cloak at the same time and their hands met. Juss felt a lightning bolt arc between them, but knew it had to be the product of his lustful imagination as they were both wearing leather gloves.

She jerked her hand away and he took the cloak and held it up for her, her eyes cast down as she turned and allowed him to lay the heavy garment on her slim shoulders. Juss caught a whiff of her scent mixed with that of wool and fur. He knew it must be his imagination, because she smelled just like strawberries.

Christ. He needed to take himself in hand or he'd make a bloody fool of himself.

He picked up her two bags and strode toward the door without speaking.

Charles took the bags and fit them in the rear luggage box while Juss helped her into the carriage and then settled across from her.

"Here." He handed her one of the three heavy lap robes his butler had been wise enough to include.

"Thank you," she said, arranging the heavy robe over her lap.

"Lift up your feet," Justin said, tucking two of the heated bricks—which were still hot enough to almost burn through his gloves—beneath her small boots.

Her eyes went wide as he took her leather-clad ankles and lowered her feet onto the bricks and she was breathing hard when he looked up. Juss knew it was because of his touch, but whether she was shocked, disgusted, or aroused, he wasn't yet sure.

"Oh," she said, her remarkable coral lips curving into a smile and her eyelids heavy with bliss. "This is the first time my feet have been warm in weeks, Juss. Thank you." She wiggled a little in her seat, as if burrowing in.

The unconsciously sensual gesture sent enough warmth through his body that Justin didn't need bricks.

***

Well, she was here, so she might as well make the best of it.

Oona looked up to find him watching her, and her face heated—meaning her cheeks would be flushed. It was a reaction she absolutely despised but could do nothing about.

43

"Do you think we will encounter more snow?" she asked. After all, there was nothing more harmless than discussing the weather.

He gazed out at the flat gray day and shrugged. "It is cold but the sky is clear. Of course nobody can know what it'll be like in seven hours. Don't worry," he said with a faint smile. "I shan't endanger your health. If it begins to snow heavily we shall take shelter."

"I'm not worried; I was just thinking this trip must be important if you are willing to brave such unpleasant weather."

"It is," he said.

"I never asked where we were going."

"No, you didn't."

Oona sighed and he gave a low, amused chuckle, but seemed disinclined to share their destination.

"Well, if you can't tell me *where* I am going perhaps you might tell me whether it will be a big party, a small party, a—"

"There will only be five guests, plus our host."

"Who are the other guests—or is that something you can't tell me, either?"

"You won't know any of the other guests."

"Why? Because I am an impoverished drudge at a modiste shop?"

"*Ex*-drudge," he corrected with his standard smirk.

"Very droll."

"You won't know the other guests because they are men of business," he said.

Oona frowned. "Men of business and their mistresses?"

He shrugged.

"I feel as if you don't want to tell me about this house party."

"You are very astute."

"Very well. Can you tell me how long we will be there?"

"Three nights at the party, the rest is travel."

44

"Goodness, that seems a long way to travel for such a short visit."

He smiled—the smile that made her palm itch to slap him. And made other parts of her itch, as well. Oona ground her teeth; her body's reaction to this man was extremely unfortunate and she would need to be vigilant over the next few days.

"What are you thinking to turn you such a charming shade of pink?" he asked.

"You've bought my person, not my thoughts," she snapped.

His eyebrows rose, but he said nothing, which only made her feel like a shrew.

"I apologize, that was uncalled for," she said, ashamed at how grudging her voice sounded. She tried again. "You appear to have done well for yourself."

"Thank you."

"Will you tell me how all this," she waved a hand to encompass the sumptuous coach around them, "came to pass?"

"I will," he said, "And I won't even charge you for the privilege."

Oona scowled.

He chuckled. "I'm sorry, that was ill-done of me, especially after you apologized so charmingly. I won't charge you, but I'll want your story in exchange."

The thought of telling this man about her humiliating past made her cringe.

"I can see my offer doesn't appeal to you."

"I've done things I am not proud of—as must be obvious from my current situation."

"You mean being in the carriage with me right now?"

Oona couldn't tell from his expression whether her words had offended him or—

"Don't worry, you've not offended me," he said, his mind-reading ability making her more than a bit nervous. "I'm not asking you to tell me *everything,* Miss Parker, just the general outline of how you ended up in LeMonde's employ."

Oona stared into his unreadable eyes for a long moment and then nodded. "Very well, my story for yours."

"I must warn you, my tale is a long and twisty one, are you sure you wish to hear it?"

"What else have we got to do?"

"Yes, precisely. What else would we do?" His innuendo made her face heat like she was a schoolroom miss, rather than a fallen, disgraced woman.

Thankfully, he ignored her furious blushing. "After I left Viscount Venable's house so ignominiously—without a letter of recommendation—I found myself with a pregnant wife and no way to support her."

"You're *married*?"

He smiled, but his eyes were as hard as sapphires. "I am a widower."

"Oh. I'm so sor—"

"As I'm sure you know, finding a position without a recommendation is a . . . well, shall we say, *challenging* proposition. A permanent position was elusive, but I found temporary work at the few inns around Halstead," he said, naming the village that had been closest to the viscount's estate. "Unfortunately everyone knew I'd been the viscount's employee and nobody was willing to risk offending him by offering me permanent employment."

Oona would have wagered—had she been a wagering woman—that his expression was accusing, but that was ridiculous. What had Oona ever done to him?

***

Juss had to take a moment to calm himself. Something about looking at the woman largely responsible for the worst period of his life was making his temper—which he usually kept under iron control—slip.

How could she sit there looking as if butter wouldn't melt in her mouth?

Juss wanted to ask—to demand, really—if she believed she'd acted morally all those years ago. He wanted to hear her justification, whatever it was.

"I'm sorry," she said, "I wouldn't have asked you if I'd known it would be painful."

He could have told her it wasn't pain he was feeling, but a decade's worth of fury. But he bit back the ragged, pointless emotion and continued what he'd started. "I decided the only way I could find work was to move to London."

Even now—so many years later—the memory of that horrible journey made him queasy. Clara had been deathly ill and shouldn't have travelled, but they'd had no choice. He'd bought them seats on a stagecoach that was so top-heavy and overloaded it broke down mid-way to London and they'd had to walk for miles in the freezing weather, which is when Clara had taken ill.

"The journey was wretched, but London wasn't much better," he said grimly. "We lived with Clara's brother because I couldn't earn enough to pay for a roof and food. After a few weeks I accepted an offer from my brother-in-law to help him with a job moving some toff's house. It turned out I was actually helping *steal* the contents of the house—or at least that is what the constables who caught us and dragged me off to Newgate said."

"Oh no," she breathed, her posture tense, her body slightly forward. "Did you tell them that—"

Juss snorted at her naiveté, and then held up a hand when he saw her offended expression. "I'm not laughing at you," he lied. "I'm laughing at the thought of trying to explain anything when my two compatriots made a clean escape and left me holding the bag."

"What happened?"

"I expected to be hung or at least transported as the house had belonged to a well-off doctor who hadn't been amused to return home to such a fiasco, but I was lucky because the Runners talked to my brother-in-law."

"He came forward and told them the truth?" she asked. Her expression told him that Juss had reaffirmed her belief in humanity. He almost felt bad about setting her straight.

"Well, he didn't exactly come forward; he'd been arrested on another job."

Her face fell. "Ahh."

"Yes, *ahhh*, indeed."

"So they released you?"

"Not quite. I'm afraid that—after almost four months—I'd managed to get myself into trouble." He had no intention of clarifying. "They decided I needed to engage in uplifting activities like peeling oakum if I was ever going to grow out of my criminal tendencies."

She looked like she was afraid to hear his answer, but she asked, "How long?"

"Two years."

She sucked in a breath, her expression one of horror. "What about your brother-in-law?"

"Ah, well, Gazzer wasn't quite so lucky."

"His name is Gazzer?" she interrupted.

Juss couldn't help smiling; she was adorable. "Er, no. His name was Gary, but everyone called him Gazzer."

"I see," she said, her perplexed expression telling him that she *didn't* see. "So what happened to him?"

"Gazzer received one-way passage on an ocean-going vessel, which was harsh, but better than doing the hangman's dance."

"Oh, Juss, that's dreadful! What about your wife?"

"My wife died in childbed while I was in gaol."

Her lips parted and one of her small, gloved hands reached out—almost as if she wanted to offer him comfort—but it jerked back quickly at whatever she saw in his eyes.

Juss held her gaze for a long moment before continuing. "When I was released, I knew there would be no chance of ever finding gainful, *legal* employment, so I joined His Majesty's Navy, which was not choosy about sailors in a time of war. Like every other volunteer I was given a shilling and two months wages in advance. And then I was off on my adventure." He paused and then asked, "Why are you shaking your head, Oona?" He decided he like the taste of her name on his tongue, and also the way she stiffened when he said it.

"Men have far more choices in life than women but not all of them are choices I would want."

Juss was startled by her observation and didn't have an immediate response.

"It must have been frightening," she said quietly.

Her expression was so open, that, for once, he didn't taunt or mock. "Yes, it was bloody terrifying, pardon my language. I'd barely gotten my sea legs when I learned the *Ajax* was on its way to a new engagement."

Her lips curled up at the corners and the effect was beyond charming. Good God. Had he said that warming his bed wasn't part of her duties? What an idiot.

"Why do you look so diverted?" he asked.

Her eyes flickered over his body in a way that sent blood rushing to his groin. "I was just thinking that *Ajax* was tall, strong, and fearless, so it was a perfect ship for you."

For the first time in years Juss felt his face heat. Was that how she saw him? He knew he was a fine figure of a man, but he'd always thought that a woman like her—educated and refined, no matter that she'd fallen so far in the world—would view him as an unlettered behemoth. Her words were, well . . .

"Juss?"

"Ah, yes," he temporized, scrambling for his wits. "I didn't know it then, but we were headed for what is now called the Dardanelles Operation."

She nodded. "Admiral Duckworth."

"I'm surprised you heard of it."

"Why? Because women don't keep abreast of such matters?"

"Not at all, darling." She jolted at the endearment and he grinned. "I only meant the operation was overshadowed by what was going on in the West."

"Oh." This time she was the one blushing.

"To make my already too long story shorter, we were waiting for the right wind to get up the Dardanelles when poor *Ajax* caught fire, ran aground, and blew up."

She raised a hand to her mouth. "Were you injured?"

"Hardly a scratch," he confessed. "Fortunately there were no fatalities. We were divided among the fleet and I made my way up toward Constantinople on the *Canopus*. As you know, not much of anything happened before Duckworth turned the fleet and headed back out. The second time through the straights we took heavy fire and something big—I never learned what—hit me in the head and knocked me overboard."

She sucked in a noisy breath, her eyes wide.

"Do you want me to stop?" he teased. "It looks like you are—"

"Don't you dare stop; this is better than an adventure novel."

Juss had never seen her so open and enthusiastic. She'd never shown anything but a prim, judging, haughty face all those years ago. Had that been merely a defense? Was it true the servants had been after her from the start? He knew nothing about the female staff but the men had all been half-way smitten—himself

Minerva Spencer

included. Juss knew they hadn't shown their admiration in a mature fashion, but had taunted and mocked. Recalling his role in all of that made him feel more than a little uncomfortable

"Juss?"

"Hmm?" He looked up from his thoughts to find her staring impatiently.

"What happened next?"

Ah, yes, his tale of woe.

"I was captured along with an officer from another ship. He'd sustained a serious hit and the Turks weren't sure that one injured officer would be enough, so they kept the rest of us— two other swabbies like me—to use in trade. The wheels turned slowly and we were held in Constantinople for some months."

"What was it like?"

Her expression was enrapt but he knew she wouldn't like the truth—no normal human being would. Still, there were bits and pieces he could share.

"It was eye-opening," he admitted truthfully. "They held the wounded officer elsewhere and kept the three of us in with a lot of other prisoners. I met men from all over."

"I shall want to hear more about Constantinople later," she told him hurriedly. "But I want to know the rest of your story just now."

"When the time came, the Turks sent us back home on an English merchant ship." Juss's lips pulled up into a wry smile. "Luckily the captain was a kind man who dropped us off before he got to Portsmouth, where the pressgangs would have been waiting for us."

"Surely they would not have preyed on men who'd already been prisoners?"

"Oh, they would prey on Prinny himself if he wandered down to the wrong docks," he assured her. "But I escaped unscathed and received a piece of paper from His Majesty that made me more respectable than I'd been before my stint in gaol."

The carriage slowed and he saw they were approaching The Three Sisters, a very busy posting inn.

"You can't stop yet, Juss. You haven't even begun to tell me how you made your fortune."

Juss was flattered by her interest, but he wasn't exactly eager to share the next part of the story. Luckily the vent slid open and Beekman saved him.

"Do you want to stop, sir?"

"Yes. I'm a bit peckish and we can see if anyone has word on the weather ahead." It hadn't snowed yet, but the sky was a menacing dark gray.

"Aye, sir." And the vent slid shut.

She looked out the window and blinked. "We are already at Colnford. I'd no idea we'd gone so far." Her cheeks tinted lightly and he knew she'd just realized her words might be taken to mean she'd been so diverted she hadn't noticed time flying. "It must be this coach," she added. "I've never been in one so well sprung."

"Yes," Juss agreed with a smile. "It must be the coach."

Eight

They'd finished the sandwiches Juss had procured at the posting house and Oona was about to ask Juss to finish his fascinating story when he said, "I think it is your turn, now—just part of your story," His big body was relaxed, his lips curled into a half-smile, and his posture insouciant.

"Aren't you cold?" Oona asked, shivering beneath the three traveling robes she wore, in addition to the new hot bricks Juss had procured for her.

Juss smirked. "No diversionary tactics, Oona. Where are you from? Why did you become a governess? You can start with those questions."

"I have to warn you that my life is considerably less exciting than yours."

"I've been warned."

She took a deep breath and sighed. "I'm from a very small town called Hexham, which I doubt you've ever heard of."

"You are correct. Where is Hexham?"

"It is west of Newcastle, in the region of Hadrian's Wall."

"You do not have a northern accent."

"No, my father was a retired Oxford don and he was most rigid about proper English. He was quite old when I was born— my mother was a good deal younger than him. She died giving birth, so it was just me and my father until I was seventeen, when he died rather suddenly after taking chill."

"Did you have family to take you in?" he asked.

Oona chewed her lip, wondering how much to share.

He cocked his head. "Yes?"

He'd shared some painful details with her—didn't she owe him something? Not about Edward, of course, but. . . .

"My mother was a prostitute when my father met her in Oxford."

He blinked, but didn't look disgusted.

"When she became pregnant, my father married her. Of course his family shunned him after that and she had no family."

"He sounds like a good man."

Tears prickled behind her eyes and she gave an abrupt nod. "He was—the best." Oona pushed back her sadness and plunged onward. "But he was also very unworldly—at least when it came to money. A few years before he died he took out a mortgage on our cottage and gave the proceeds to one of his old acquaintances from Oxford who had some sort of scheme."

"Let me guess," he said grimly. "The scheme fell through."

His look and tone made her feel defensive. "I know you are thinking he did not do a very good job of taking care of me."

"Am I wrong?"

"Not entirely, but he made the investment because he knew that the cottage would not be enough—that I would have still needed to work."

He said nothing.

Oona shrugged. "I was young, but my father had taught me well so I looked about for governess positions. Lord V-Venable was my first interview. At that time the viscount had been widowed six months and his children were desperately in need of care. He offered me the position right after we spoke and I accepted." Naturally she turned a flaming shade of red just saying Edward's name.

He frowned and leaned toward her, his gaze more piercing than usual. "Why are you blushing?" he asked. "Did he tamper with you—force himself on you?"

"What? No! No he never forced himself on me," she retorted. "Why would you say such a thing?"

He snorted and gave a dismissive flick of his hand. "Go on. Why did you leave Compton Abbey?"

It had been so long since she'd heard the name spoken out loud—so very long since she'd even allowed herself to *think* it—that it took her breath away for a moment. She'd been foolish to have even begun telling him a story that held nothing but pain for her. Well, not *just* pain, there was Katie, of course. She bit her lip. This had been a mistake.

Make something up, the cool voice in her head ordered. *You taught English composition, surely you can spin a creditable yarn?*

Lie? Could she really just—

"Oona?"

The single word scattered her thoughts like a cat tossed among pigeons. Lord. Had her name ever sounded as good as it did on his tongue?

"I left to accept a position with a school friend." She paused. "Let me retrace my steps a bit." *So that I might lie more effectively.* "I'd attended a girls' school in Oxford that was run by a friend of my father's. After my father died they offered to allow me to spend my final year with them even though I didn't have the tuition. I refused because I knew I would need to work and I might as well face my future sooner rather than later. My school friend was a year younger than me and in the same position. She'd taken a position at a newly opened academy which needed an English instructor and the position paid well."

"So you simply pulled stumps and went to . . . ?"

"Bath, a town already blessed with its share of girls' schools."

"I take it by the fact you are in London the school did not prosper."

"No. It closed two years ago after the owner died suddenly and her niece, who inherited the school, shut it down without even finishing out the term. So then I was without a reference, except for Lord Venable's, which was too old to be of any use to most employers." It was a tangle of lies, but there was nothing she could do to make it any better at this point.

"I see."

Oona knew what he was thinking—he was wondering about what she'd so foolishly told him in a fit of confusion and anger: that she was a fallen woman with no references. Why had she ever said that?

Because your tender feminine wits were scrambled by his distracting masculinity.

Oona scowled at the taunting voice.

"Ah, our luck has run out, it seems."

She looked up from her mental chaos to see that he was staring out the window.

"Snow," she said foolishly.

He nodded, the corners of his full lips turned down.

Oona took the rare opportunity to study his face without having to bear the brunt of his burning gaze. He was unfairly handsome. Even the wrinkles and lines and few gray hairs served to make him more attractive—distinguished, even. Something she never would have believed he could look when she thought back to him as a younger man. Oh, he'd been handsome, but there'd been nothing distinguished about it. It had been raw sensuality that he'd emanated a decade earlier.

He turned and caught her staring and the grim set of his jaw softened into his mocking half-smile.

"What will we do?" she asked in a breathy voice when it seemed he was contented to stare at her.

56

He pulled out a gold pocket watch. "It is barely three o'clock. We shall press on for a while and see how things are." He looked at her and smiled. "Was the job you had with LeMonde your first in London?"

Oona frowned at the change in subject but could see by his expression he'd not be diverted.

"No. I had a teaching position in a household where the master and mistress were willing to believe my tale of woe about the school and pleased to have me because I'd taught for a peer, no matter how many years ago." *That, at least, was the truth.*

"Ah. A Cit, I take it?"

"That is not a word I would use."

He grinned at her chastising tone. "Go on."

"To make a long, dull, story shorter," she said, paraphrasing his words, "the lady of the house came to believe I had designs on her husband. And her son."

His face hardened into an expression of disgust that gutted her and Oona dropped her gaze to his feet, her face burning. Why had she thought he would look any different?

"Let me guess," he said, "They both chased you around their vulgar Cit house and became angry when you rebuffed their advances?"

Her head whipped up.

"What?" he said.

"It's just—well, I'm surprised. The woman at the employment agency didn't believe me." It had been worse than disbelief: it had been scorn.

Juss snorted. "Come, come, Oona—we were both servants together." He scorched a trail of heat across her with his hot eyes "I know what it is like for servants—especially female servants—and their masters."

The words hung between them and he held her captive with the intensity of his gaze, his expression . . . knowing.

The question was, just what did he know?

***

Juss left the matter of masters and female servants alone for the moment, afraid he'd not be able to keep a civil tongue on the matter. So they rode in silence, both of them consumed by their own thoughts.

It was perhaps a half hour later when the vaults of heaven opened and the scene outside the window became a solid white.

"My goodness," she said softly.

"Indeed."

Beekman opened the vent. "I can't see a thing, sir."

"That was Anston a ways back, wasn't it?"

"Aye."

"Then we can't be far from Falk Hill."

"We may 'ave just passed it—should I turn around?"

"That would be a bloody trick right now, wouldn't it," Juss demanded. "Even if we could manage it, what if somebody else came barreling along while we were stretched across the road?"

"All right, all right, guv. What then?"

"Keep on, but more slowly. Stop if you see anything decent, even a farmhouse."

"Aye, sir." The vent slid shut.

Blast and damn and bloody hell!

Juss looked up to find the woman staring at him, her expression. . .

"You're enjoying this," he said in amazement.

Her delicate pink lips curved into a grin. "Well, it is rather exciting to be traveling in a blizzard."

He snorted. "Let's hope you find it exciting when we are freezing to death in a snow drift."

"It is one of the oldest roads in Britain, surely we'll have no trouble finding shelter."

But forty-five minutes later, when the carriage had slowed to a crawl and the last of the daylight had drained away, she did not look so excited. Instead her smile had disappeared and her smooth brow was deeply furrowed. Juss felt like a brute for what he'd said earlier.

"Oona?"

She wrenched her worried gaze away from the window.

"Don't panic yet," he teased gently. "Somebody once told me this is one of the most ancient roads in Britain."

Her lips twitched into a faint smile.

The vent slid open. "There's a light just up ahead—but it seems to be moving."

"Moving? Good God," Juss muttered. "Well, you'd better give it a look—it could be some poor dumb bas—" Juss glanced at Oona. "Er, it could be another traveler who is lost."

"Aye, guv."

"Do you really think it is somebody lost in this storm?" she asked once the vent had closed.

"I don't know," Juss said. "But I'm guessing we're about to find out."

Nine

It *was* somebody out in the blizzard, but they were not lost.

"He's looking for *what*?" Juss asked again, just to make sure he'd heard correctly.

"Er, 'e's lookin' for 'is cat, sir," Beekman said, his tone of disgust communicating his thoughts on the matter.

They'd turned off the main road to follow the light—a man with a lantern—a short distance down a branch road and it would be impossible to turn back at this point.

"'E says 'is 'ouse is just ahead, sir. A small farm, but we're welcome to stay." He hesitated and then added. "'Is name is Jonathan Cantrell and 'is wife's name is Mary. 'E seems like the a right 'un, guv."

Juss nodded. "All right. Tell Charles to take the rear coach lantern and help the man find his *cat*—and that you and I will come help them once we've settled the horses."

Juss would have helped the man find his bloody cat right now—it was the least he could do for an offer of shelter—if he'd not had Oona with him, but he hardly wanted to send her into an unknown house alone.

"Aye, guv." Beekman trudged off and Juss pulled up the window.

"He must be a nice man if he is out in this searching for a cat."

Juss snorted. "Or perhaps he's just crazy."

Her chuckle was unexpected. "Have you never had a pet?"

"No."

"That is very sad," she said with exaggerated pity.

"Are you mocking me, Miss Parker?"

"Perhaps a little."

"Did *you* ever have a pet?"

The carriage started moving and she settled back in her seat, the pile of rugs on top of her barely shifting.

She gave him an assessing look. "Well, sort of."

"A sort of pet?"

"You aren't allowed to tease."

"Oh? But I do it so well."

"Yes, I *know*."

The atmosphere in the carriage was suddenly charged, like the air before an electrical storm. Because Juss had lighted both lamps in the carriage an hour before he saw her pupils flare. Predictably, his body responded to her involuntary sign of desire, the blood rushing south, a wave of warmth flooding him.

Christ. It would be a bloody miracle if he managed to keep his hands off her.

But he'd given his word, so he forced a smile and said, "Tell me about your pet. I promise I won't tease. Much."

"We kept a few hens where we lived and one of them, Mimi, was just lovely."

"You had a pet chicken," he said, and then held up both hands when she scowled. "Sorry, not mocking."

She looked unconvinced.

"Tell me how one has a pet hen? My own experience with hens is limited to—" he stopped, deciding she wouldn't like any mention of axes and chopping blocks. "Never mind about that. Tell me about, er, Mimi." He could tell by her smile that she was pleased that he'd remembered the name.

"Mimi would sit on my lap and take bits of biscuit from my hand; she'd follow me around while I gardened; she'd come beg at the kitchen door for scraps—things a dog or cat might do."

Her eyes had softened and her smile was gentle as she remembered her hen. Juss wanted to tell her that he'd follow her around and eat from her hand if she smiled at him that way. Luckily he said nothing of the sort.

He shook himself. Lord, he was becoming a sentimental fool in his dotage.

Just then the carriage shuddered and slid to the side before grudgingly rolling to a stop.

"Is this it?" Oona asked.

They peered out the window, barely able to make out a building beyond, the snow too thick to see much more than a big, dark shape.

Rather than use the window when Beekman came to talk to him Juss opened the door and hopped down, the snow almost to his knees.

"The old fella said the barn around back could take the carriage, guv."

Juss nodded. "You get the team settled and then bring the luggage to the house. We'll go help Charles after."

"Aye." Beekman turned and trudged to the head of the team.

Juss held out his hand. "Come. I'll carry you."

Oona opened her mouth—no doubt to demur—but then glanced at his legs. She hesitated and then placed a small hand on his shoulder and lowered herself into his arms.

As he recalled from a few nights before, she was as light as a child. But despite her spencer and cloak he could feel her soft curves; she was not shaped like a child.

"Pull a couple of those rugs onto yourself and then take the lamp," he ordered. If his voice was a tad bit husky that was probably due to the cold, wasn't it?

***

Oona hadn't been so warm since the *last* time she'd been cradled in Juss Taylor's arms. Thankfully she was so bundled up he wouldn't notice either her body heat or the inconvenient quivering that came over her whenever he touched her—even through four or five layers of clothing.

She forced her attention toward the small farmhouse just ahead. The closer they came to it, the more she could see little details, like the charming rolled roof and the glossy black shutters that only allowed slivers of light. There was a covered porch and Juss set her down gently. It was lucky they'd brought the lamp because the one in the holder beside the door was dark. Likely the couple only used this entrance for guests, which they'd not expected tonight.

Juss knocked and they waited.

"It seems very nice," she said softly, her words accompanied by fluffy clouds of steam.

"It seems very small," he said, glancing down at her. "As much as it might pain you, I think you'd better be Mrs. Taylor."

Oona glared up at him, her body thrumming at the meaning in his heavy-lidded gaze. "If you are trying to warn me that we shall likely have to share a room, I had already discerned as much. I am hardly a—"

The door creaked open to expose a wizened old woman who was even smaller than Oona. As she blinked up at them Oona saw her eyes were clouded almost white. She smiled uncertainly. "Yes?"

"Mrs. Cantrell?" Juss asked.

Her expression shifted from confusion to fear. "Did something happen to Jon—"

"No, no, your husband is fine," Oona hastened to assure her.

64

"He is out with my footman looking for your cat, ma'am. He is fine," Juss reiterated. "I'm afraid we got caught in the blizzard and—"

The old lady opened the door wide. "Of course, of course—you must be frozen half to death. What am I thinking to keep you standing outside—come in, come in." She squinted up at them, her expression one of awe as she looked all the way up at Juss. "My, but you're a big fellow."

Juss chuckled and shut the door behind him. "I am Justin Taylor and this is my wife, Mrs. Oona Taylor."

Oona felt a frisson of excitement at the sound of her name coupled with his.

"Welcome, welcome," Mrs. Cantrell said. "I'm afraid I don't see as well as I used to, so I have to use this old thing," she tapped her cane on the floor. "I wasn't expecting visitors so the parlor is as cold as a grave. But the kitchen—"

"The kitchen sounds wonderful," Oona assured her.

Mrs. Cantrell smiled with relief. "You can take off your coats in there and get warm by the stove." She turned and began stumping her way toward the back of the house, leading them through a series of cold, dark rooms. "I apologize for all this gloom but the light doesn't help me much so I don't light candles when it's just me and Jonathan here. Usually my daughter and her husband would be here, but they went to see his family since they won't be with them at Christmas this year, so it's just the two of us."

"You're all alone?"

"We have two young folks from town to help, but I daresay they'll not be here tomorrow with all this snow."

"Oh, that smells delicious," Oona murmured as they approached a doorway with light leaking out around the edges.

"I was just getting some baking in when I noticed Winnie wasn't laying in her favorite spot near the stove." She opened the door and Juss sucked in a deep breath

"Mince pies?" he asked hopefully.

The old lady chuckled. "And two apple." She set her cane into a holder by the door, her actions more confident in a room that was clearly her domain. "Go warm yourselves," she gestured to a huge stove shimmering heat. "I'm going to put the kettle on."

"Thank you for your hospitality," Juss said, lifting Oona's cloak from her shoulders and hanging it on a peg before removing his own scarf and coat. "I don't think we could have made it to Henley tonight."

"Oh goodness gracious!" she said, turning away from the tea pot, which she was filling with tea leaves. "You're a good hour away on a clear day and probably four or five on a night like tonight."

Juss pulled a chair closer to the stove and gestured to Oona. "My coachman was having difficulty finding the road. He was lucky he saw your husband's—"

Sounds came from the small room just off the kitchen.

"Is that you, dear?" Mrs. Cantrell called.

A slight, bent figure appeared in the doorway, stomping heavy boots on the straw matt. The only part of his face Oona could see were twinkling sky-blue eyes and fluffy white eyebrows.

"It's me, Mother."

Mrs. Cantrell moved with remarkable speed toward him, her hands finding his scarf as if they had eyes of their own. "Jonathan, did you—"

"I didn't," he said, as he tugged off his thick woolen mittens. "But the young man found her."

"Oh thank goodness." Her slender body sagged with relief.

"You go sit down, Mother," he urged gently as he took the ends of his long scarf from her hands and unwound it to expose a face so crisscrossed with age you could hardly see his features.

Mrs. Cantrell straightened suddenly. "I'm in the middle of making tea for our guests, Jonathan Cantrell. Plenty of time to sit and chat after."

Jonathan Cantrell grinned at Oona and Juss, unchastened. "After sixty years you'd think I'd know not to come between Mary and her tea."

Sixty. Years.

Just how old were these people? And why were they alone?

Oona met Juss's gaze and knew he was thinking the same thing: this man might not have made it back home if Charles hadn't been there to help.

Mr. Cantrell's gnarled hands were surprisingly nimble as he unbuttoned the big wooden toggle buttons on his coat. "That's a nice young man you've got working for you, sir. He carried Winnie inside his coat and said he'd bring her from the barn once he'd helped your coachman with the horses."

"I'm pleased he could be of some assistance," Juss said. "My wife and I are grateful for your hospitality."

The old man waved a dismissive hand. "Dreadful night to be out on the road." He shuffled over to hang his heavy coat. "Smells like heaven in here, Mother," he said, dropping into a chair with a sigh.

"I suppose you'll be wanting some pie along with your tea."

Jonathan winked at Oona. "I'd not say no to that."

"Why don't you show Mr. and Mrs. Taylor to Lucy and Donny's room? I'm sure Mrs. Taylor would like to wash up before tea."

"Oh, you don't—" Oona began, not wanting to disturb the old man just after he'd sat down, but he was already pushing creakily to his feet.

67

"Follow me," he said, moving so slowly toward the door Oona wondered if they'd be back in time for tea.

"My daughter and her husband are off gallivanting with my two granddaughters," Mr. Cantrell said as he led them through a different part of the maze-like house. "They have our old room as Mother and I are no longer good friends with steps." He paused at the bottom of a narrow staircase.

"We can find our way," Juss assured him, "You needn't make the trip."

"Are you sure? Mother will skin me alive if I don't get your fire going."

Juss chuckled. "I'm perfectly capable of starting a fire, sir."

After only a little more debate they were left to find their new quarters on their own.

There was only one room at the top of the stairs. One cozy room with a tiny cupboard, two chairs, fireplace, and one bed.

Juss crossed the tiny room and opened a narrow door that held a washstand and necessary.

They both sighed; thank the Lord for that, at least.

The sound of voices down below made them both turn. "That must be Charles with our luggage," Juss said to her. Whatever he saw on her face made him smile. "How are you liking your adventure so far, Mrs. Taylor?" Oona glanced at the bed, and he chuckled. "You go wash up first. I'll start the fire."

Like a coward, Oona scuttled into the tiny room and closed the door behind her, collapsing against it.

One. Bed.

Oh my.

Ten

Juss rolled onto his right side, but it wasn't any more comfortable than his left. His knees were bent because the space between the foot of the bed and the fireplace wasn't quite long enough, thanks to a cupboard jutting out of the wall. It would probably be just as comfortable sleeping *inside* the cupboard.

Fortunately the wooden floor had a carpet, albeit not a particularly thick one.

"Are you asleep?"

He glanced up at the bed, even though the light from the fire was so faint he couldn't see his hand if he held it three inches in front of his face.

"No. Are you?"

She laughed and he smiled like an idiot, glad it was dark.

"Can you believe they are both eighty-one years old?"

"They are remarkably spry."

"I don't think I've ever seen a married couple who like each other so much." Her voice was heavy with admiration.

"Yes, even after sixty years," he agreed, rather amazed by the old couple himself.

"Juss?"

"Hmm?"

"How did you become so successful?"

He stared into the darkness, torn. He'd never told anyone how he'd accumulated enough money to buy his first property—a step that had led to another and then another, as he learned he had a sort of genius for determining which part of London to invest in.

"It's not a very uplifting tale."

"Oh." There was a long pause, and then, "You don't have to tell me if you don't want."

Juss didn't tell her that he already knew that, that he hadn't needed to do *anything* he didn't want in years—not since he'd earned enough money to tell anyone who ordered him to do *anything* to piss off.

But he wanted to tell her, even though he would not come out of it in a very positive light. He didn't want to look at his reasons for that. Not now.

"Once again I found it difficult to find a job that paid enough to afford a roof *and* food," he said. "I'd met a man while I was held in Constantinople, a Prussian who spoke better English than I did."

Oona chuckled and the sound warmed him.

"Dieter and his brother had inherited a pottery in Cologne and saved their money to buy the building next to it to expand. Before they could do so, they received an offer for the building that was almost twice what they'd paid, so they moved their pottery to a new location and still had money left to buy another building. That's when they decided that buying and selling properties was more lucrative than pottery. They were doing exceptionally well when Dieter was pressganged one night on his way home from their pottery. He'd not been able to get word to his brother and had been gone for three years by the time I met him."

"That's dreadful! His brother probably thought he was dead."

Juss nodded and then remembered she couldn't see him. "When I was released I sent a letter for Tomas, so his brother knows the truth."

"Oh. That was very kind of you."

"You sound surprised," he said wryly, not waiting wait for an answer. "I thought about Dieter's story a lot, but couldn't figure out how to accumulate enough money to even begin. Certainly that would never happen scraping by with part-time work at inns." He took a deep breath, held it, and then released it slowly. "I knew the name of the man my brother-in-law had worked for. I knew he paid well because the work was both dangerous and illegal." He paused, but she said nothing.

"I finally decided to go see him. Needless to say he was not a trusting fellow." Juss didn't tell her that Crazy Eddie Mayer was the most suspicious, unstable, dangerous man he'd ever met. Nor did he share the fact that Eddie had beaten the shit out of Juss—or had his henchman do it, rather—and then kept him locked up for two weeks before actually talking to him.

"After some consideration Eddie decided to hire me, but I would begin at the bottom." Juss shook his head; what bloody awful days those had been. "To put it bluntly, Oona, I was a petty criminal. I stole, fenced, and enforced for Eddie."

"Oh."

He smiled bitterly. "Oh, indeed. I worked in that capacity for six months or so, steadily moving up, until I became one of his personal guards—the most trusted of his men." Also the most likely to irritate Eddie in some harmless fashion and end up dead, thanks to his proximity to the maniac.

"That was both better and worse: better because I didn't have to work the streets, but worse because Eddie liked to throw his weight around." Or have Juss do it for him, which earned him a reputation as one of the most dangerous men in that part of London. "It was perhaps a year after I'd started for him that he began a turf struggle with another gang—one stronger than his—that ended very badly for Eddie and most of his men. It was

71

just dumb luck that Eddie had sent me to deliver a message at the time of the attack."

"Did they—were they—"

"Dead, all of them."

There was a long moment of silence, when Juss was tempted to tell her about the boys' school he'd started—his way of making amends for his criminal past. But the thought of puffing off his good deeds left a sour taste in his mouth.

"What happened next?" she asked, her tone curious rather than disgusted or judging.

"Eddie paid the men who guarded him well, and we lived and ate for free because he kept us with him. That meant I'd saved most of my money. I didn't have enough to buy an actual building, but I had enough to invest in a small bakery." He didn't tell her that it was a business Eddie had all but ruined by squeezing it for "protection" money.

"Even with investing in the bakery I had enough money left to play the 'Change."

Nobody had been more surprised than Juss when it turned out he was a bloody wizard when it came to trading. It was a skill he'd never expected to find in himself, and one that made him a very, very, very wealthy man.

"And so you bought more properties?"

"No, I wasn't good at what Tomas and his brother did. I was more successful with business investments. I've since purchased a few places—the one on Cork Street, for example—but I generally keep them as I've not got the knack for buying and selling them." He shifted his body to find a more comfortable position, failing to do so but banging the top of his foot against the bed leg in the process. "Bloody hell!" he muttered under his breath.

"Juss?"

"Hmm?" He rubbed the top of his foot, grateful his toes were too frozen to feel much pain.

"Are you comfortable down there?"

"Very droll, Oona."

"There is room enough for two in this bed."

Juss froze and then said, "I beg your pardon."

She sighed. "Come up here. It's foolish to stay on the floor when there is all this room."

"Are you sure?" His cock was certainly sure.

"Yes, of course."

There was no *of course* about it, but Juss didn't have the decency to turn her down. He stood and spread the blanket he'd been using over the bed and then hesitated. "Which side do you want?"

"Oh. Well, I don't know. Do you prefer a side?"

He'd not slept in the same bed with a woman since Clara, preferring to visit his lovers and leave once they'd finished their business. He couldn't recall what side of the bed he'd slept on. Hell, he could barely remember Clara's face after so long.

"I'll take the right side," he said, just because he was on the right side.

He heard movement followed by a silence that seemed to pulse, and then lifted the covers and climbed into the warm, fragrant spot where she'd been lying.

Juss lay on his back, the blankets pulled up to his chin, as he tried to ignore the insistent erection that would not let him sleep, even if he *had* been tired.

***

Oona was experiencing difficulty controlling her breathing, which was coming in rapid, shallow bursts. The truth was, she already regretted her impulsive offer. Not that she believed he would do anything untoward, but her body was reacting to his— even though it was motionless—in a most disturbing way.

"Regretting being a Good Samaritan?" His voice was rich with amusement.

"No, of course not."

He chuckled. "Will you be able to sleep?"

Oona smiled in the darkness; it *was* an amusing situation. "Oh, eventually. I think. I don't normally go to bed so early." That was the truth, but not the *whole* truth.

"No, I can't recall a time when I've been tucked in by eight o'clock, either."

Oona felt the bed shift and he must have turned on his side because the next time he spoke, his voice was much louder, even though he was speaking softly. "Are you tired, Oona?"

Her brain seemed to melt a little at the low, sensual heat in his voice. "Uh."

"You're *uh*?"

"I'm not tired," she managed in a hoarse voice.

"I have a question for you."

Oh God. She knew what—

"You mentioned that you were a fallen woman. What did you mean? Did the men you mentioned—your employer and his son—impose upon—"

"No, it wasn't that," she said hastily. "It was another man—I believed him when he said he would marry me." Saying the words was like pouring salt over a wound she'd believed scabbed over a long, long time ago. "But it turned out that all he wanted—" Oona bit her lip.

"Shhh," he murmured. "I'm sorry. I didn't mean to open old wounds."

"No, it's all right," she said. Oddly, that was the truth. It was cathartic to speak about it after all this time.

"Did you love him?"

It was not a question she thought a man like him would ask— he did not seem the sort who even believed in love—and it surprised her. She turned onto her side; this conversation was too interesting to not be face-to-face, even if they could not see one another very well in the near darkness. "I thought I did."

"But you were wrong?"

Again he surprised her. Who would have thought he would ask such a thing? And why did he even care?

"I loved like a younger person loves, with emotion rather than one's brain."

"That is an interesting distinction. I would have thought love was always emotional."

"You've never—" she stopped aware of the delicate direction in which she was headed. The last thing he would want is somebody—a virtual stranger—probing the subject of his dead wife.

"Been in love?" He didn't sound angry or sad, just contemplative. "No, I don't believe so. I can sense that you are surprised," he said, and Oona didn't deny it. "My marriage was one of necessity rather than love. Although of course I cared for my wife." He paused and then asked, "Tell me, if you could do it all over again—change the decisions you've made—would you do it?"

It would have been easy to say yes—and that was certainly her first thought. But then she saw Katie's precious face. "No."

"Really? You wouldn't go back and make a different choice? One that didn't cause you pain?"

"That seems like an easy question to answer, but one small change would mean an entirely different life—wouldn't it?" And it would certainly mean no Katie.

He chuckled.

"What?" she asked.

"We have become philosophical."

Oona smiled. "Would you go back and change your decision?"

"No," he answered without hesitation. "I agree with you—one different fork in the road would have led to a different destination."

"And you like your life." I

"And I like my life," he agreed. "Tell me," he said, "You said you had plans this week. What were you going to do if you weren't here? Or is that too personal a question?"

"I was going to visit friends." It wasn't entirely a lie.

"Ah."

Oona had no idea what that meant. As much as she knew about Justin Taylor's past, she still had no idea of what he thought. She rolled onto her back and stared into the blackness overhead. What a strange journey this was turning out to be.

Eleven

Oona woke with a start, her eyes darting around the dimly lighted room, struggling to recall where she was.

In bed at a farmhouse. With Juss.

Her head whipped to the right, but the bed was empty.

She pushed back the covers and put on her dressing gown, a garment Juss had chosen, its creamy lace and silk making her blush just looking at it.

Oona scoffed at her foolishness. She'd slept with the man and he'd clearly been able to resist her, silky lacy garment or not.

She pushed aside the heavy drape and sucked in a breath. It was a magical wonderland, the pale lemon sunrise causing everything in sight to sparkle as if diamonds, rather than snow, had fallen—*continued* to fall. Something moved in her peripheral vision and she turned to see Juss and his barrel-shaped coachman slogging through the snow from the big white barn.

Naturally, Juss glanced up and caught her, his mouth curving into a grin. Oona dropped the curtain, and immediately felt foolish. He'd seen her in her dressing gown last night, why was she behaving like a schoolroom miss?

You spent the night in bed with him and you are disappointed he made no move to touch you.

Oona growled at her stupidity and found her watch: it was a little after seven.

After washing with the still warm basin of water Juss must have brought, Oona headed down to the kitchen, feeling more than a little foolish in her second travelling costume, which was even fancier than the first. But it was all she had that was clean.

The first person she saw upon entering the cozy, delicious smelling kitchen was Mrs. Cantrell.

"Good morning dear." She squinted at Oona. "My, that's a lovely outfit."

Oona flushed. "I'm afraid all my other clothing is in the other carriage."

"Aye, your husband told us."

Oona glanced at the bubbling pots on the stove and Mrs. Cantrell's floury hands. "What smells so delicious?"

"Steak and kidney pie, a few loaves of bread, and some tarts. But you don't need to stand in the kitchen, Mrs. Taylor. Mr. Cantrell has warmed up the parlor and I can bring you tea and breakfast."

"Please call me Oona. And I'd prefer to eat in the kitchen, if you don't mind having me."

"Oona—that's a beautiful name. Well, you can call me Mary. Would you like ham and eggs, dear?"

"Just tea and some toast, I think."

"You're like me," Mary said, putting the kettle on the stove. "I can't eat a heavy meal in the morning or I'll sleep all day."

Oona gestured to the big bucket of potatoes. "I can peel those for you."

"Oh no, you'll get your pretty clothing dirty."

"I see a second apron over there—is that your daughter's?"

"Aye." She looked doubtful, her cloudy eyes sweeping over Oona's person.

"Please? I'd like to help."

It took a bit more cajoling, but Oona was rolling out pastry when Juss came in from the cold an hour later.

"Well, look who's up," Juss teased, so vital and masculine and gorgeous with his rosy cheeks it was almost painful to look at him.

"I've been up and laboring for hours, I'll have you know."

"Have you now?" Juss stripped off his gloves and tossed them into his hat, his startling blue eyes on her the entire time. "Where is Mrs. Cantrell?"

"I persuaded her to take a nap—after fifteen minutes of arguing—convincing her I had things well in hand."

"What are you making there?"

"Pastry for more pies."

"Mmm, I like the sound of that." He unwound his scarf and then removed his coat, which was glistening with rapidly melting snow. "Well," he said, once he was down to his clawhammer and buckskins and looking better than a man had a right to do. "I'm afraid the men who were supposed to help Jonathan with the animals didn't show up, but the three of us were able to get them all fed."

"Would you like some tea?"

"Yes, please."

"Shall I make some for Mr. Cantrell, is he coming along soon?"

"Jonathan is in the land of Nod."

"In the *barn*?"

Juss dropped into a chair, his long legs stretched out in front of him. "He's got a smithy out there—that's what they do here. Or what his son-in-law does. Mr. Cantrell has a comfortable chair not far from the forge where I suspect he spends a good deal of time napping. The farm is not their true means of support, just to earn a bit extra. Which is a damned good thing because tracking down and feeding thirty sheep was plenty."

Oona smiled as she rolled out the dough with the huge maple wood rolling pin.

"You look at home in a kitchen," he said.

"Well, I've never had servants, so I should."

"Until now," he corrected.

Oona frowned and then said with exaggerated comprehension, "Ah, that's right. I meant I didn't have servants until we married."

He grinned. "So, what kind of pie are you making, Mrs. Taylor?"

"Steak and kidney."

"My favorite." He glanced at the eight pies and multiple loaves of bread that were already on the baker's rack. "Who the devil is she making all this food for?"

"Apparently there was to be a dinner and dance at their church this evening."

"Ah, well, I don't see that happening."

Oona paused in the act of crimping the crust. "So you think we will be here for a while?"

"I should think so. Even if it stopped snowing right this minute the roads would likely be impassible at least for another day."

"You shall miss your house party."

His expression, which had been easy and smiling, tightened. "I shall be there for at least a day, which is really all I need."

"You would drive the rest of the way only for a day?"

He nodded slowly.

"Why is your destination a secret?" she asked, an unpleasant sensation unfurling in her stomach at his intent, almost avid, look.

"It's a surprise." He suddenly stood. "I've changed my mind about the tea," he said as he strode toward the door, catching up his coat and hat. "I'm going to go and explore a bit."

Oona stared as he stepped out into the snow—which was now coming down diagonally.

What had *that* been all about?

Twelve

Between meals shared with the Cantrells and helping the older couple with their chores—Juss outside and Oona in the kitchen—he wasn't alone with Oona until after supper, which they ate at the uncivilized hour of *five*.

It was clear that last night had been unusual for the Cantrells and that their usual bedtime was closer to six-thirty than eight.

Juss realized the older couple wouldn't go to bed until he and Oona excused themselves, which is how they found themselves closeted together in the small bedroom at five minutes to seven.

"Do you want to use the changing room first?" Oona asked.

"I'll never be able to sleep if I go to bed this early."

"Me either." She sighed and sat down on the bed, her nightclothes in her arms. Juss lowered himself onto the only chair and stared at her profile, sharp and delicate and remote.

"Why are you angry with me?"

The words were so low he almost didn't hear them.

He opened his mouth to deny it, but then closed it, too disheartened to lie. All day long he'd wrestled with this problem as he'd wandered around in a blizzard. He'd created this trouble for himself and could only come up with one solution—and it was not one that would be comfortable.

The truth was that Juss *liked* this woman and he was about to drag her into a situation that would be unpleasant. What did it matter if she'd told on him a decade ago? Her actions might have gotten him discharged, but Clara had been pregnant and would have been fired regardless of what Oona said. So, really, it didn't matter.

"I know it was you who told Venable."

She squinted. "I beg your pardon?"

Justin made a noise of irritation and stood. "I'm sorry I even brought it up. It hardly matters after all these years."

"I have *no* idea what you're talking about."

Juss scowled; he'd not expected such deception from her—he'd believed she was more honest than that. "I know you saw me fucking Clara."

She flinched at the vulgar word and then shot to her feet. "I can't—I don't—"

"I *know* it was you. Are you trying to tell me that you didn't understand the consequences of your actions?"

"*What* actions?"

"Dammit, Oona! You told Venable that you'd seen us that day."

There was a long silence. "You think I told the viscount about that?" Her voice sounded strange—almost trancelike.

"Didn't you?"

"How could you think that?" Before he could answer she made a sound like a feral cat and then threw her wadded up garments at his head.

Juss caught them easily. "What? Why are you playing the victim?"

She marched toward him—which only took a few steps in the tiny room—not stopping until he could smell the distracting scent of strawberries. And then she hauled her arm back and slapped his face. Hard.

Her action seemed to surprise her more than it did him and she took a step back, both hands covering her mouth, her eyes wide. "I'm so sorry, I'm sorry," she whispered through her fingers. "I don't know what—"

Justin moved his jaw from side to side and rubbed his cheek. "You pack a good wallop."

"I'm so—"

He held up his hand. "Yes, you're sorry—I understand that. But I take it from your reaction that you *weren't* the one who told Venable."

She dropped her hands and shook her head.

If it wasn't her, then who the hell—

"I'm guessing it was Lucy who told the viscount about you and Clara."

"Who the devil is Lucy?"

"She was one of the parlor maids. A tall, thin—"

Juss snapped his fingers. "A dark-haired girl with a face like a rat."

She winced. "That is unkind."

"But true."

She sighed. "She did look a bit like a rodent. Normally I wouldn't give voice to such an unkind thought but she had an unpleasant personality."

"Why do you think it was her?"

"It was she who came to me that day and told me to look in the linen cupboard. I had no idea what she meant but I assumed it was one of the children up to something again." She shrugged. "So I opened the door and—" Her mouth opened and closed several times. "How did you see me? You were—" her cheeks flared red and she couldn't finish the thought.

"Why would she have told you to do that?"

The look she gave him was one of mute misery and it was Juss's turn to gape.

"I can see you understand," she snapped, even though he had no intention of pursuing the subject.

"Er—"

She held up a hand. "Don't bother. Every woman in that house—from fifteen to fifty—was mad for you. Why should I have been any different?"

Juss didn't think she really wanted an answer to that question and wisely kept his mouth shut.

"How did you know it was me?" she asked.

"Clara saw you."

"Which meant she must have seen Lucy, too," Oona pointed out quite logically. "So why did she only tell you about *me*?" Her expression was bitter and confused. "Why would she have done that? Mention me but not Lucy?"

Juss met her furious gaze; well, she'd told him a mortifying truth . . .

"Because she knew I fancied you."

Juss had to smile at her stunned expression; did the woman not possess a looking glass? Why was she so bloody surprised that he'd liked her?

"Oh."

"Clara must have thought she'd put paid to any positive thoughts I might have harbored for you—not that it made any sense since I'd never see you again," he muttered, so angry at himself he could hardly speak. Christ! What a bloody fool he was. Ten years angry at a woman who had nothing to do with it. And even if she had—what kind of idiot harbored such a grudge?

"If you were angry with me, then why am I here? Why did you give me this job? Why are you paying me so much?"

Juss wasn't accustomed to being so wrong, or looking so much like a fool. But he owed her the truth.

"Because the house party is at Compton Abbey."

He'd read about all the color draining out of somebody's face, but never actually seen it. He rushed forward when she staggered backward, but she pushed him away.

"Don't touch me." Her expression of revulsion was far more painful than the slap had been. "What were you going to do when you got me there?"

"I remember the way Venable ate you up with his eyes," Juss said. "I wanted to show him that not only did I survive, but I had somebody he'd wanted."

"As your *whore*."

"Yes," he admitted, his head so hot he was sweating. "As my whore."

Her magnificent green eyes sparked. "Did you arrange to have me discharged from my job?"

"*What*?" he demanded. "No! Of course I didn't. How could you think such a thing?"

She gave an ugly laugh and Juss flushed even hotter. "Fine, point taken," he admitted. "I haven't exactly behaved in a forthright, gentlemanly manner. But I would *never* stoop to having you fired."

She waved her hand dismissively. "And what is your punishment for him?"

"He is below the hatches and I hold the notes to Compton Abbey"

She snorted. "You *are* clever—and efficient. In one action you could have revenge against the two of us—the person who tattled and the one who discharged you."

Juss had to admit that, when spoken out loud, it did sound rather. . . juvenile, if not downright stupid.

But then he remembered Clara and what Venable had done to her. He'd never told a living soul Clara's secret, but he did not want Oona to keep looking at him the way she was currently doing.

"I agree that my behavior has been reprehensible." Juss flinched at her bitter laughter. "But I haven't told you the entire story."

87

"There's *more*? What else did you have planned for us—for *me*? A public stockade? A stoning?"

"I know you don't owe me anything, but let me tell you the rest of the story."

For a moment he thought she would tell him to go to hell.

But then she dropped gracelessly onto the bed, fixed him with a dead-eyed stare, and said, "I'm listening."

***

Oona felt like she was in some kind of nightmare: all of this had been revenge. He'd never wanted to help; he'd never liked her. He'd only wanted—

"I now gather that you never heard why I was sacked?"

Oona threw her hands up. "How would I have? None of the servants ever spoke to me. All I know is that one day you were there, and then you were gone."

He shook his head and muttered something beneath his breath. "He called us both before him, one at a time, and told us he didn't tolerate that kind of behavior. And then—" he ground his teeth. "And then he accused me of getting not only Clara pregnant, but a woman who'd worked there and left six months earlier—do you recall Jenny Linton?"

"A slight, dark-haired kitchen maid?"

He nodded.

"*She* was dismissed for becoming pregnant?"

"Apparently, although that was the first time I'd heard about it."

"So you hadn't—"

"No, I barely even knew Jenny."

"Did you tell him that?"

"What was the point? He might not have been wrong about Jenny, but he was right about Clara—or at least that's what I thought at the time."

A sick feeling was growing inside her. "What do you mean?"

88

"I won't deny that what I'm about to tell you is self-serving. It doesn't justify my behavior toward you, but perhaps it will help you understand what I was thinking."

She crossed her arms. "Go on."

"Clara's child wasn't mine, it was Venable's."

Oona couldn't breathe.

"She was two months pregnant and decided I would make a good father." He shrugged. "Being young and stupid and apparently incapable of simple addition, it didn't occur to me that the child was coming far too soon until the midwife said something to me not long before I went to gaol. When I confronted Clara, she told me the truth. I couldn't fault her—she'd been scared and alone. If we'd not been caught together I probably would have married her and we would have stayed working at Compton Abbey and I would have been none the wiser."

"Did she say—that he—"

"He didn't force her, but she said he was persistent and persuasive and finally she just gave in."

Oona knew exactly what Clara meant. *Exactly*.

He sighed heavily and she looked up. "I know the bastard knew the child was his—along with poor little Jenny's. But of course there was nothing a mere groom—a disgraced impoverished one at that—could do. I'm sorry for what I almost did to you, Oona. But Venable?" His jaw tightened and his expression made her shiver. "I *hate* him." His blue eyes burned, the pupils tiny specks. "All those years I couldn't find a job because *he* had discharged me without a reference for a child that was his—" He stopped, his jaw so tight she could see the muscles ticking beneath the skin. "Clara might have still died had we had a home and ample food, but then again she might have been fine. I might have had ten children by now. Instead she died at the age of nineteen in miserable circumstances because of *him.* "

The only sound in the room was the fire crackling.

"You will take his house?"

"I will take his house, his land, *everything.*"

Oona could not argue with him, nor did she want to. Viscount Venable was a man who took what he wanted and let others pay the price; Oona knew that better than anyone. She looked at Juss, who was staring at her with a strange expression.

"What is it?" she asked.

His mouth pulled into a half-smirk, but this time it looked self-mocking. "You never knew I fancied you?"

"Of course not. I thought you all disliked me—you especially. You always teased me so dreadfully whenever I came to the stables with the children."

"I was young and stupid." His face broke into a sudden, disarming grin. "Of course I'm now older and perhaps even more stupid."

Oona couldn't help smiling.

He stood and came toward her, holding out his hands.

Oona put her hands in his before she even considered her actions, and he pulled her gently to her feet.

"I'm sorry I believed ill of you," he said, his eyes roaming her face as if he were searching for something.

"I'll admit it hurts, but after what happened to Clara?" She gave a tired shrug. "Well, apology accepted."

"Thank you," he whispered, releasing one of her hands and brushing her jaw lightly with the back of his fingers. "I still remember the first time I saw you," he said in a voice that didn't sound like him—a voice that almost dropped her to her knees. "You were the most beautiful woman I'd ever seen." Oona made a mortifying gulping sound. "And so *proud* and stiff and haughty," he said with a smile, his fingers not ceasing their delicious stroking.

"W-why didn't you say anything?"

"You were beyond my reach, weren't you? A governess and a groom? Not very likely."

Oona could have told him it was far more likely than a governess and a viscount, but wisely kept that to herself.

Instead she told him the truth. "I wish you would have said something."

His hand froze, his pale eyes darkening. And then his mouth lowered over hers.

Thirteen

Juss's palm slid around to hold the back of her head, his lips caressing hers, his teeth nibbling, and his tongue invading— his actions smooth yet dizzying.

This was not Oona's first kiss, but it was certainly the first kiss of this sort.

He was gentle, but something about the way he entered and stroked her—as if he wanted to consume her—was beyond wicked.

Edward's kisses had been swift, rushed, and closed-mouthed, as if they were something to be gotten through quickly.

Juss kissed her with languorous thoroughness, as if kissing her was his new avocation and he could kiss her all day and night.

There was so much of him and he engulfed her with his big body without overpowering her, making her feel safe, cherished. When was the last time she'd been held by another person other than Katie? And even that had been months ago.

Oona heard a moan and knew it was her, but she didn't care. She burrowed into his arms, pressing her body against his erection, glorying in the knowledge that he'd become so hard for *her.*

A growl of approval rumbled from his chest and he trailed kisses from her mouth to her ear.

"I've thought about you so bloody often over the years. I couldn't believe it when I saw you standing there that night—right beneath my not insignificant nose."

Oona laughed softly, too thrilled by his words to speak.

"I want you, Oona." He ground himself against her belly, the action crude and primitive and so very arousing. "If you want me to stop, tell me now, because—"

"I want you, Juss."

He made a primal sound of pleasure and dropped to one knee, taking her booted foot in one hand.

"Take off your coat and unbutton your dress," he ordered, his big fingers methodically working the buttons of her ankle boot as efficiently as a button hook.

Oona's own hands were shaky and unresponsive and he'd already removed her boots and she was barely out of her coat.

He stood, staring down at her with a look of raw possession, his hands moving on his coat, which was tight enough that getting out of it was an erotic contortionist show for Oona.

But not as erotic as the long hard ridge that distorted his tight leather breeches. His hand slid across his erection and he squeezed himself, the muscles in his hand and forearms flexing in a way that made her swallow. When his hand released his arousal Oona's eyes jumped up to find his smile one she'd never seen before—sensual, needy, and cruel.

"Come, come, Miss Parker. You'll never get that coat off at this rate."

She fumbled so badly with one of the buttons that she snapped the thread and it skidded across the floor. He chuckled and leaned forward, sliding his powerful hands beneath her shoulders and lifting her onto the bed with as much ease as Oona had lifted Katie when she'd been a baby. But Oona was no child and his strength caused an insistent throbbing between her thighs that made her legs weak.

94

"I'll finish for you," he whispered against her ear, and then nipped her earlobe, making her jump. Oona whimpered at the sensation of his night beard scratching against her tender skin, his fingers working blindly but surely on the few buttons that ran down her back.

His mouth stopped at the base of her throat and he licked and sucked on her pulse before lowering his lips to the swells of her breasts and groaning. He took her hand and lifted her to her feet while he pushed the gown off her shoulders, his dark gaze flickering over her stays and chemise.

"You're so lovely," he muttered, turning her around swiftly enough to make her head spin, his hands working on her laces. "I've had dreams about you, Miss Oona Parker," he whispered heatedly, his hips pulsing against her lower back, his organ impossibly hard. "And the things I did to you in those dreams—" he broke off with a wicked chuckle and spun her to face him, seizing her mouth with a ferocity that left her breathless. "How is it that you taste like a strawberry, Oona?"

Before she could answer, not that she *could* answer, he shoved the stays over her hips, pulled the chemise over her shoulders, and then tossed her onto the bed, where she landed with a squeak, wearing only her stockings and garters.

"You're perfect," he hissed, reaching over his back to grab a fistful of shirt and pull it over his head, revealing some perfection of his own.

Oona's mouth fell open and he grinned down at her, running one hand over his astoundingly defined abdomen before pulling open his fall and then pushing down breeches and smallclothes with one shove.

"Oh my." Oona had supposed that men differed in penis size as well in all other regards, but. . .

He gave a low laugh, the action causing his muscles to shift and tighten in fascinating ways. Once again he grabbed himself, and Oona watched in stupefaction as he gave himself several ruthless pumps before taking her knees and pushing them apart.

When she sucked in a shocked breath and tried to resist he paused and looked up from her exposed sex. "I'm going to make love to you with my mouth." He laughed outright at the noise she made. "Did your lover never pleasure you that way?" he asked, his nostrils flaring as his eyes flickered between her hips and eyes.

"N-no," she stuttered, which she seemed to be doing quite a lot. She'd liked lying with Edward, but he had been efficient and speedy and would have already come into her at this point. He'd certainly never suggested something so outrageous.

Juss lowered himself while pushing her wider and wider. "Open for me, Oona, I want to see you."

She couldn't resist him—not because he was using force, but because he was looking at her with an expression that was reverent and hungry.

She startled when his thumbs slid up and down her swollen, sensitive lips; nobody but her had ever touched her down there, but Juss's fingers were exploring her with an eager confidence that sent waves of anticipation and pleasure ricocheting through her body.

And then he opened her and she jolted and bucked. "Justin." The word came out half groan, half whisper, and she breathed in ragged gasps.

"What is it, love?" he cut her a glance, but quickly looked back, as if he were transfixed. "So pretty," he crooned, and then lowered his head and covered that most sensitive part of her with his hot, soft mouth.

***

Juss massaged her with his tongue, smiling against hot, slick skin when she cried out and her hips bucked. It was a good thing

Mr. and Mrs. Cantrell were both slightly deaf as he was going to make Oona scream tonight.

He brought a hand up to her entrance and slid his middle finger inside her while he sucked.

"Oh, Juss."

He released her with a soft sucking *pop* and began to work her with his hand. "Do you like it," he asked, pumping her in slow, deep strokes.

"Please," she whimpered.

"You want more? You want my mouth on you?"

"Mmmph." She nodded jerkily, her head tipping back, her pelvis lifting in silent entreaty. Juss gave a soft laugh of triumph and closed his mouth on her, working her ruthlessly toward her climax. He moved to her entrance when her peak became too sensitive, replacing his finger with his tongue. She was even tight around his tongue so he slid in first one and then two fingers while she writhed, scissoring gently, stretching her snug passage and getting her ready.

"Shall I make you come?" he asked in a voice rougher than gravel, his fingers pumping her, harder now.

She shuddered at his crude words. "Yes, please. Juss . . ."

She was so sensitive that he'd barely begun before she was bucking and grinding into his mouth, her small hands laced into his hair and holding him steady while she used his mouth for her own pleasure.

He needed her right bloody now.

Juss pushed onto his knees while the waves of pleasure wracked her body, lifting her legs over his forearms and bringing her hips toward him. "Take me in your hand, Oona—guide me inside your body," he rasped.

She complied with shaky, clumsy urgency and he pulsed his hips gently against her, but not enough to breach her, just stroking her slick softness with his sensitive crown, teasing, pushing in a little more with each stroke until his fat head was inside.

He groaned. "You feel so good. I won't last, Oona, I'm sorry. I won't—" Juss's cock took control of his body and he entered her in a long, hard slide, not stopping until his balls rested against her spread sex. He hesitated a moment, vaguely aware he'd taken her harder than he'd intended, wondering if he'd hurt her, wondering if—

Her sheath tightened around him. And that was all it took.

***

Oona imagined it was what being caught in a hurricane or electrical storm must be like—a force of nature that could not be stopped.

His powerful hips drummed savagely, his strength alone an aphrodisiac. Oona remembered how to tighten her inner muscles and then relax them the way Edward had told her to do and Juss shuddered and groaned.

"Yesss," he hissed his eyes closed, his expression one of bliss.

The two men were as different in bed as they were in every other way. Juss was earthy, enthusiastic, and generous—just as he was in the rest of his life. Never had she guessed a man could—or would want to—give her such pleasure. A pleasure she had only ever given herself in the past.

"Oona," he rasped breathlessly, capturing her with his slitted gaze, his teeth gritted in a snarl, and his nostrils flaring. "Going to—" he grunted, his thrusts becoming jerky and uncontrolled. He stopped with shocking suddenness and pulled out of her, pumping his long, slick shaft once and then twice before his body went rigid.

"Oh God." The muscles of his chest and abdomen became even more defined with each spasm, the cords of his throat strained and distinct as hot ropes ribboned over her belly and breasts.

Oona could not look away. He was so big and ruddy, the veins that ran up and down his shaft were visibly pulsing each time he spent. He was an erotic work of art, hard and slick and lost to his passion.

The last shudder produced barely a drop from the small slit and he groaned, a massive shudder wracking his huge frame as he dropped down beside her, his body shaking the bed so hard that the Cantrells, who slept below them, must be staring at the ceiling and wondering if the roof had caved in.

He pushed himself almost drunkenly off the bed onto his feet and then bent to snatch something from the floor—his shirt. Oona frowned. Was he getting dressed already? What was he—

"Here." He lowered the shirt over her stomach.

"No, you'll—"

"Shh," he murmured, mopping up all trace of his spend.

"You'll ruin it," she said, almost more breathless at his careful cleaning than she'd been before.

"Then it will be ruined," he grumbled. "The water in the basin is too damned cold and those towels are as rough as tree bark." His hot eyes burnt over her body. "And you should never have anything but the finest, softest silk touching your beautiful skin."

Oona gaped.

He gave his signature smirk and then used the shirt to dry himself before tossing it off to the side and collapsing onto the bed beside her.

"Oona."

Never had anyone said her name with such utter and thorough satisfaction. He reached an arm over her and grabbed a handful of bedding, pulling it over her body, tucking her tight to his muscular form from shoulders to hips and then heaving a huge sigh.

It was a moment before she realized that he'd simply fallen asleep, his arm like an iron band around her body.

Oona couldn't help laughing—a silent shaking laugh that would not wake him—she was wide awake and he was unconscious. But then he'd done all the physical work, hadn't he?

Her breathing quickened at the memory of his muscles flexing, his hips pounding, his glorious—

Katie.

The joy she'd been feeling leaked out of her like water from a cracked pitcher.

Tonight he'd looked at her with desire and even affection in his eyes. But that would change in a heartbeat when he found out about Katie; then his expression would be something else entirely.

If Justin Taylor ever learned that Oona had not only been Venable's lover, she'd also born his child, he'd look at her with the same expression he'd worn when he'd spoken of Viscount Venable: with eyes pulsing with loathing and hate.

Fourteen

Juss woke as dawn was breaking. The light through the gaps wasn't gray, but a warm yellow: it must have stopped snowing. He turned his head and looked at Oona, who lay sleeping on her side, facing him. One of her hands rested on his bicep and one of her feet was against his calf. Her magnificent auburn hair was spread across the pillow in wild spirals and her lips were slightly parted as she breathed evenly.

He'd taken her again last night, the second time just as intense, but slower, more thorough and intimate.

Juss peeled back the heavy comforter and feasted on her naked body. Her nipples were dark pink and large on her surprisingly full breasts. His mouth watered and he leaned forward and flicked one with the tip of his tongue, smiling when she murmured in her sleep, the sensitive disk of flesh puckering. He took the nub into his mouth and sucked and she groaned and shifted sensuously.

"Juss." Her voice was sleep-roughened.

He released her stiff peak and slid his hand over the soft swell of her belly, through the darker auburn curls of her sex, his cock throbbing painfully when she opened herself to welcome him.

"I want you again," he said, his middle finger sliding between her wet, swollen lips. "Are you too sore?"

She shuddered and rolled onto her back in answer, her legs spreading wider.

Juss chuckled as he pushed onto his knees, his hand still on her, his finger thrusting deep into her tight passage.

"Fuck!" he ground out the vulgar word, amused when her sheath tightened around his finger like a vise.

The light was pale but it was enough for him to see her beautiful face as he knelt between her thighs, pushing them wider with his knees while his free hand went to his stiff rod. He thumbed the freely leaking slit, slicking his shaft while she watched him through lazy eyes, her hips pulsing against his pumping hand.

"Good God you're beautiful, Oona." He thrust out his hips, his fingers curled tightly around the base of his stand, the action displaying his size to advantage. "Do you want this inside you?" He smirked—preening for her just like a cock for a hen.

She touched his crown with one finger, rubbing the work-roughened pad in the bead of sticky liquid.

Juss hissed harshly looking from her circling finger to her face. She was biting her lower lip, her eyes wide, watching her hand.

"Taste me, Oona."

Her lips parted with shock but she hardly hesitated before bringing her slick finger to mouth. She gave a soft grunt as she sucked off his juice, her eyes narrowing.

"Bloody hell," he snarled, dropping his weight to one hand, while the other positioned himself at her opening, and entered her with a brutal thrust.

***

Oona didn't recognize the woman she'd become as she writhed and thrashed and moaned beneath him. She just *wanted* too much to care what he must see. He'd dropped to one elbow and then reached between their bodies while his hips pounded her with punishing force.

"Come for me," he ordered, his crude command and dancing finger driving her with shocking speed toward her pleasure.

His words shoved her over the edge and her body clenched and rippled around him.

"Ah, God!" he cried out, bucking hard before jerking out of her and finishing himself, his fist a blur, until the only sound or motion in the room was their mingled breathing.

He gave a deeply contented groan and then rolled onto his back and reached down beside the bed.

Oona chuckled. "Your poor shirt."

He laughed weakly. "It has done its duty," he said, cleaning her before himself. "I think it will be allowed to retire now." He tossed it onto the floor and then, unlike last night, turned on his side toward her rather than falling asleep. "That was very rude of me last night—to fall asleep both times." He propped his head on his hand, reaching out to tuck a tangled lock of hair behind her ear.

"I must look like I've been yanked through a dozen hedges."

"No, just half-a-dozen."

She scowled. "It's not fair," she said, allowing her eyes to move over him with a boldness she could scarcely credit.

"Hmm?" he said, his fingers combing her hair, an odd smile curving his lips. "What's not fair?"

"It's not fair that you look perfect—your hair hardly mussed, while I look like—"

"You look like a goddess—a sated, well-pleasured goddess."

She gaped at the odd, yet satisfying, compliment and he mirrored her expression.

Oona laughed and he grinned.

"There, that's better," he murmured, his hand caressing.

Her face heated under his almost adoring stare. "It looks like it's sunny," she said, needing to say something.

"Yes."

"What are our plans?"

He stroked her throat, his broad, powerful hand making her feel delicate and small. "My plan is to take Jonathan's sleigh to Henley and engage either a horse or a chase for the rest of the journey."

"Are we leaving right after breakfast?"

He leaned forward and gave her a lingering kiss, her lips parting for his tongue eagerly, like a welcome visitor. Oona brazenly explored him, running her tongue over his teeth, the inside of his lips.

"Mmm," he groaned, and then pulled away, his hand on her shoulder. "Look what you've done." He glanced down and Oona saw that his breeding organ had once again begun to thicken. She laughed.

"Witch." He kissed her hard and then leaned back, his expression becoming serious. "You will stay here until the road is clear. Beekman will take you back to London."

"But—"

He laid his index finger across her lips. "No. I don't want to take you to Compton Abbey." His soft, full lips hardened. "I don't want you to come within miles of Venable. Even if you *had* told him about me that day it doesn't mean you deserve to be soiled by his presence. No woman does."

Oona's eyes clouded at the hate in his tone.

"Hey then, what's this?" he asked when a tear rolled down her cheek. "Don't cry, love."

She shook her head, although she didn't know at what or whom or why.

"Oona?"

She looked up to find an expression on his face she'd never seen: uncertainty.

"I like you, Oona." He frowned and his jaw worked, as if he were having some sort of argument with himself. "I like you a great deal. I don't think I'm mistaken in thinking you might like me—at least a little?"

She gave a watery snort and shoved his chest, which did nothing. "Of course I like you," she said thickly. "I wouldn't have—what kind of a—"

"Shh-shh," he murmured, wrapping his bulging bicep around her and pulling her tight to his body. "Don't cry, darling."

The endearment just made her cry harder.

"I want—well, I want—*Christ*," he growled, his hard chest rumbling against hers as he held her painfully tight. "I want *you*, Oona. I know it's too bloody fast, but I feel like—" He gave a growl of frustration. "I thought I was good with words," he said wryly, "But I guess that's only when it comes to pounds and pence. What I want to say," he hesitated. "What I want to say is that I want to see you again when this business with Venable is done. Beekman will take you back to London and I've got a lovely little place where you could stay while you considered, er, things."

He wanted her to be his mistress. Oona squeezed her eyes shut; God, it was the most tempting offer she'd had in her entire life.

But then Katie's face rose up before her. To be with Juss would be to deny her daughter. Already she only saw Katie mere days every few months. She couldn't pretend she didn't exist.

"Oona?" He pulled away and his hand tipped her chin up, until she couldn't avoid looking at him. His expression was uncertain. How had she managed to make such a powerful, confident man look so vulnerable?

Oona swallowed; she refused to hurt him now—not when they could still spend a few more hours together. No, tomorrow or the day after or the day after that would be soon enough to take the light from his eyes.

Oona forced a smile onto her face. "I will go back to London," she said, careful not to lie. It was a small, ultimately pointless, distinction, but one that was important to her.

"And you will let me take care of you—just until you make your decision?"

"Yes. I will let you take care of me until I've made my decision." *I'm sorry, Juss. So sorry.*

His lips curved until he was grinning. "I shall make you a happy woman, Oona. I promise you that—well, you won't regret it." He pulled her close. "I—" His embrace grew painful and the very air around them shimmered with expectation. But then his arm loosened and his body seemed to deflate. "I look forward to it," he said lamely, his voice so sad she wondered what it was he'd really wanted to say.

***

Juss was barely a half day away from Compton Abbey when it started to snow. Again.

The carriage slowed down when the sky opened up, creeping along until it finally turned off the road and then ground to a halt in front of a tiny posting inn.

Juss knew what the postilion would say before he even opened the window.

"Sorry, guv, but we ain't allowed to keep goin' in this wevver." He cut a significant look at the sky, as if to draw Juss's attention to the thick white flakes falling like leaves. "We can wait 'ere and if it clears up in an hour, mebby go a piece. But ovverwise," he shrugged. "Well, I'm finkin' we'll be spendin' tonight 'ere."

It didn't clear up in an hour, nor two or three. Juss took one of the four rooms the tiny inn had to offer and parked his arse in a chair, his eyes riveted to the scene outside the window, his brain somewhere else.

He'd been a bloody fool to leave Oona at the Cantrell's farm yesterday morning. Not just because of the foul weather—which had meant yet another night in a roadside inn last night—but because of the way she'd looked when he'd kissed her goodbye. She'd looked deeply, profoundly, sad, even though her mouth had been smiling. Juss had seen it, but had been too much of a bloody coward to ask what was bothering her.

Because you know what was bothering her: You, a man so bent on revenge you would leave her alone to pursue it. You should have gone with her back to London. You are a fool.

Juss couldn't argue with that.

Not long after he'd left her—maybe not even an hour—he'd suddenly realized his hunger for vengeance had disappeared, replaced by another hunger: for Oona.

Like a sleepwalker who'd awakened from a long nightmare, he couldn't understand what had been so compelling about destroying Venable—a man who was already doing a fine job of destroying himself—that he would leave a woman he'd been thinking about for *years*.

There was no point in returning to Compton Abbey, a place he certainly had no desire to occupy or even own—even though he did. No, he would call in the notes through his man of business and then put the place for sale. And that would end this dismal chapter of his life.

Juss smiled like an idiot as he gazed unseeingly out the window. And then he could return to London—to Oona—and begin another chapter. One that would hopefully lead to a more satisfactory ending to his story.

Fifteen

Oona looked up from her needlework, her eyes immediately going to Katie's strawberry blond curls. It had been three weeks since she'd come to Ightham, a tiny village not far from the school that Katie now attended as a day student, but Oona still could not believe that she had her daughter to herself—not just for a two-day visit, but permanently.

"How much longer, Mama?" Katie asked, looking up from her work.

Oona glanced at the clock on the mantel. "Only until three, darling."

Katie groaned. "It's Christmas Eve! I'll wager none of my friends from school are doing sums today."

"I hope you will *not* wager, Katherine Anne."

"Oh, Mama."

"Fifteen minutes," she said firmly, smiling to herself when Katie heaved a huge sigh but turned back to her remaining schoolwork.

Some days her daughter's presence was the only thing that made it worthwhile to get up in the morning.

As hard as she tried to forget him, Justin Taylor had taken up residence in her brain—and heart—and seemed in no hurry to leave. It was foolish and self-destructive to allow herself to think of him as she'd most certainly killed any chances she'd had with him after leaving him in such a deceptive, underhanded way.

After spending one more night with the Cantrells, the road had been clear enough to head south. She'd arrived in London, collected her small cloth bag of possessions from her landlady, and took a hotel for the night. She'd spent most of that evening thinking about the money Juss had offered her. By the following morning she'd decided to keep four hundred pounds for the four days she'd spent on the journey and returned the rest along with a brief letter—the hardest letter she'd ever written. All Oona had said was that she was grateful for their time together and his generous offer of money.

Juss would be hurt and rejected, but he was a gorgeous, powerful, wealthy man and any pain he felt would likely pass quickly. At least she hoped he wouldn't suffer. Not like she was suffering. But she had the added pain of knowing she had left a man she loved; yes, there was no denying that this much agony could only mean love. The shameful truth was that Oona would have been his mistress in a heartbeat if matters had been different.

She felt a familiar prickling behind her eyes that heralded tears and dropped her gaze to her idle hands. She couldn't cry—not in the middle of the day. That is what nighttime was for: yearning for Juss and crying. Because it certainly wasn't for sleeping.

"Mama?"

Oona looked up through bleary eyes. "Hmm?"

Katie had put aside her quill and pushed up from the table where she'd been working on her sums, which she hated. "There is a man on a magnificent horse coming down the drive."

Oona jabbed herself with her needle, yowled, and stood so abruptly her tambour slid to the floor; she knew who it was before she rushed to the window.

"Oh." Oona clutched her throat, drinking in the sight of his powerful, elegantly clad body like he was a pitcher of cool water and she was a parched wanderer in the desert. Which was not far from the truth.

"Who is it and why would he be coming here on Christmas Eve?" Katie asked, her gray eyes crinkling at the corners as she gazed up at Oona. Her eye color was the only feature she'd taken from her father—at least when it came to looks. But when it came to behavior, Katie had Viscount Edward Venable's persistence and charm, and then some. Her father had been able to charm the birds from the trees—or at least a governess into his bed—by making Oona feel as if she were the only woman in the world. Katie was *almost* as skilled at charming her way out of chores.

"Mama?"

"You stay here," Oona said, waiting until Katie nodded before moving toward the door, her hands unconsciously going to her hair. She swallowed several times, hoping to generate some moisture in her suddenly bone-dry mouth, to no success.

Quit acting like a fool and get out there!

Oona jerked open the front door and found him only a few feet away.

He stopped, his jaw dropping in a way that would have been comical if she wasn't in such physical pain looking at his beautiful face.

"Oona."

The sound of her name on his lips made her flushed and dizzy. "What are you doing here, Mr. Taylor?"

He recoiled—either at the cool tone, formal greeting, or both—and his face darkened. "I came to see you, obviously."

"On Christmas Eve?"

"Yes. On Christmas Eve." His beautiful eyes were stormy—angry and sad and something Oona couldn't decipher.

She smoothed her skirt, unable to stay still. "Didn't you receive my letter?"

His lips twisted into a bitter smile. "You mean the one with three sentences and three banknotes?"

Her face heated.

"Yes, I received that."

"Then why are you here?"

He took a stride toward her and she stepped back.

He stopped, his expression one of barely suppressed fury. "What the hell happened between the time we said goodbye and three days later when I returned to London?"

"You were back in three days?" she blurted.

He brushed aside the question. "I deserve an answer. You told me you would be in London, that you would be wa—" His hot blue gaze slid to something over her shoulder and his jaw sagged.

Oona closed her eyes and groaned. "I thought I told you to stay inside, Katie," she said before pivoting to face her daughter.

"I'm sorry, Mama. But I just wanted—"

"You have a *daughter*!"

Oona opened her mouth but before she could answer Katie stepped forward, her forehead furrowing, her expression mulish—a look Oona had to admit she'd inherited from *her*. "Don't shout at my Mama." She stepped beside Oona and slid her hand around her waist, her nine-year-old body quivering to do battle on Oona's behalf.

Juss shook his head. "Good God—it's a little Oona."

"You shouldn't take the Lord's name in vain," Katie scolded. "And my name is Miss Katherine Anne Parker."

Juss's knowing gaze met Oona's. "I'm sorry, Miss Katherine," he said, his eyes going back to Katie. "You are correct, I should not say such things." He bowed, "I am Mr. Justin Taylor, a friend of your mother's." He pulled off his black leather riding glove and extended his hand. "It's a pleasure."

Katie's face lit up like a pyrotechnic display at this unprecedented demonstration of male gallantry. She gave him her small hand with as much dignity as a queen and dropped a graceful curtsy, her eyes sparkling up at Juss in a way that said she was half-way enslaved already.

And then both sets of eyes, one gray, one blue, turned to Oona.

"Well," she said, hiding her fear and excitement behind a grudging tone, "I suppose you might as well come in and have tea. Before you go."

***

Juss couldn't stop staring at her as she led him into the house, stopping first in a small parlor to settle her daughter at a table covered with pages of childish handwriting.

"I'm going to take Mr. Taylor into the kitchen for a moment. I want you to finish your work, Katie."

"And then we'll finish making the buns for the carolers?"

"First I shall bring you a cup of tea and a biscuit."

The little girl's eyes were fastened on Juss in a way that was adorable.

"But *Mama*, I want to take tea with you and Mr. Taylor. And maybe he could help us with the buns—and the carolers?" She gave Juss an ingratiating smile that would be devastating the male population for miles around in a few years.

"Katie." Oona did not raise her voice, but her daughter complied—albeit grudgingly—to the soft authority.

Oona shut the kitchen door and then spun on her heel, her arms crossed tightly across her body. "What are you *doing* here?"

Juss took a step toward her and she took a step back. This time he didn't stop; he kept walking until her back was against the kitchen door, her eyes and mouth wide as she stared up at him.

Juss claimed her mouth with the pent-up hunger of days. She hesitated for a split second—that felt like an eon—and then thrust her hands into his hair and launched her body into his arms, their teeth clicking painfully as their tongues fought, the coppery tang of blood baptizing their violent passion.

Juss's head spun as he gripped her soft, fleshy bottom, holding her pressed to his erection while he savaged her mouth, Oona giving as good as she got.

Far too soon she came back to herself and pushed away. "Put me down," she hissed, her lips swollen, slick, and bruised.

It was an agonizing struggle to force his arms to comply with her command.

Once she was at liberty, she brushed off her skirt with shaking hands and then pointed to a small table, her entire body trembling. "Sit," she ordered, spinning on her heel and stalking toward the stove.

Juss dropped into the chair and drank in this evidence of her lust for him, even if she felt nothing else. Which he simply could not believe.

"Tell me why you are here," she demanded as she put the full kettle on the stove and then turned.

"I would have been here sooner but it was a bloody miracle that I found you," he snapped, recalling the frantic, almost mad sickness that had come over him when he'd returned to London to find her gone.

"I looked for you at your dreadful lodgings and learned you'd paid up before even leaving. I went to LeMonde—oh, by the way," he said, "the thief was apparently one of your coworkers—a woman named Marie?"

She gasped. "Marie? But she was the one urging Madam to be kind to me."

Juss shrugged. "Guilty conscience. Anyhow," he shook himself, getting back to the point, "LeMonde had nothing about you except that address." Juss let all his frustration show in his frown and growling tone. "You just bloody disappeared without a trace—after what—" he broke off and scowled at her. "Good God, Oona! How could you be so cruel?"

Her face crumpled at his accusation and she raised her hands to her flaming cheeks.

"Oh hell," he muttered, lunging to his feet so fast the chair hit the wall. When he took her in his arms she melted against him. "*Why,* Oona?" he asked as he stroked her delicate shoulders, holding her close while he showered kisses on her beautiful hair, inhaling the intoxicating scent of *her*; of strawberries.

"Because Katie is—"

"Katie is?"

"She is Venable's daughter."

"Yes, that is what I assumed," he soothed, staggering back when she thrust away from him.

"*What?*"

The door to the kitchen opened a crack. "Mama? Is aught amiss?"

"Katherine Anne Parker," Oona began, but the door snapped shut. Oona whipped around and glared up at Juss. "How did you *know* that?" she demanded, her hands on her hips.

He shrugged. "Just by looking at her." He grimaced at whatever he saw on her face. "You likely don't want to hear this, but she looks a lot like Venable." Juss took a step toward her but she moved back. He shoved a shaking hand through his hair. "Lord, Oona. What the devil is wrong with you? Are you still in love with him?"

"*What?!*"

They both looked toward the door at the sound of feet thundering on the other side, but the door remained closed.

"Are you?" he demanded.

"*No,* of course I'm not in love with him."

"Then why the hell did you disappear? Do you hate me that much? Is that why—"

She lunged toward him and punched him in the arm. "I *love* you, you—you."

"Ow!" He grabbed his shoulder. "What was that for?"

She shook her head back and forth, her expression agonized. "I don't—I don't *know*," she wailed.

Juss grabbed her, holding her struggling body in an unbreakable embrace. "Oona, stop it, love. You'll hurt yourself. And—and I love you and don't want you hurt."

She froze. The room was silent but for the pounding of his heart in his ears and then, "You l-love me?"

He squeezed her until it had to hurt. "Why do you think I'm here?" He released her and she gasped in a deep breath as he took her stubborn little chin and forced her to look at him. "If you love me, why did you leave?"

"Because—" she jerked her head toward the door, tears dribbling rather than streaming now.

"Because of Katie?"

She nodded.

"But. . . *why?* Did you think I would judge you for having a child outside of wedlock?" he asked in disbelief.

"*His* child."

He frowned and then it dawned on him. "Do you really believe I'd take out my dislike of Venable on a *child?*" He dropped his hands from her body and stepped away from her. "Is that what kind of man you think I am?"

She opened her mouth, but nothing came out, her eyes raw.

Juss ground his teeth, hating that he was the source of her anguish. "I guess we're even now. I believed you would get me sacked and you believed I could be so petty."

Her chin wobbled and then she launched herself at him and he closed his eyes as he held her tightly. "She is your daughter,

Oona," Juss said, blinking rapidly for some odd reason. "How could I not love your daughter when I love you so much it hurts?"

Epilogue

Oona could not pull her eyes off Katie as she swirled around the dancefloor, gazing up at the young man who gracefully led her through her very first waltz as a married woman.

"Are you sad?" A strong arm linked with hers.

Oona glanced up at Juss, who towered beside her, breathtaking in his formal black-and-white attire. At forty-two he was more handsome than ever, his thick, inky hair silver at the temples, but his eyes the same brilliant blue.

"A little," she admitted, leaning against his now familiar, but still intoxicating body. "But I always knew she would fly away some day."

"Well, she's not flying far, at least," he said with a chuckle. "And I trust Anthony more than any other young man I've ever met," he added.

Oona had to agree. Anthony Burke had begun life at the bottom and worked his way up under Juss's tutelage. He was seven years older than Katie, but the two had really been a case of love at first sight. Oona was grateful her oldest daughter was going to a man as strong, loving, and dependable as Juss.

Of course Justin Taylor was also arrogant, conceited, high-handed, dictatorial, and a half-dozen other things Oona couldn't recall at the moment. The fact that they were both strong willed had meant the last ten years had often been tempestuous. They'd argued, fought, and then made up with the same fervor they seemed to do everything together. Oona sometimes wondered if the passion in their marriage was to make up for those ten years between their first and second meetings.

"What are you thinking about, sweetheart?"

Oona smiled and pressed herself against him, even though they were in public. "You, of course."

He chuckled, the sound smug and satisfied. "I *know* you are thinking of me," he said. "But *what* exactly are you thinking?"

"How much I love you."

His body stiffened and Oona couldn't help smirking at the reaction those three words still had on this powerful man after all these years.

"You'd better," he said gruffly.

Oona's gaze slipped back to Katie. "I'll miss her, Juss."

"Me too, sweetheart." He rubbed her shoulder with his big warm hand.

"The house will feel empty."

"You mean other than Julian, Frances, and Albert?" Juss asked ironically. "Have you forgotten about our *other* three noisy and demanding children?"

Oona smiled. "All right, so it won't seem empty."

"I was thinking we might go someplace for a week—just the two of us, maybe somewhere in the country."

Oona tilted her head and looked at him. He was smirking in that wicked way of his, his eyes hooded and glinting.

"Oh? Where would we go?"

"I'm afraid I can't tell you that."

Oona bit her lip to keep from laughing. "Hmm. A trip to the country—I'm not sure. . ."

"I would make it worth your while," he murmured.

"Is that right?"

"Mmmm hmm."

"Are you sure you could afford me? I'm *very* expensive."

He sucked in a breath, his gaze so intense it felt like there were only the two of them in this room full of hundreds. "I remember the day you accepted my rude, vulgar offer as if it were yesterday, Oona. But I feel like it's long enough ago that I can confess I would have paid at least five times as much to have your company for a week."

"As it seems like a time for confessions, I have to admit I was a trifle disappointed in your much vaunted business acumen that day."

He barked out a laugh. "Oh, and why is that, darling?

Oona grinned up at him and then—quite deliberately— winked. "Because, you foolish, wonderful man, you could have had me for free."

■■■

Thank you so much for reading *A Second Chance for Love*!

If you enjoyed Juss and Oona's story, then keep reading for a sneak peek at

THE MUSIC OF LOVE ...

Chapter One

Portia Stefani pulled her gaze from the moonlit countryside beyond the carriage window and stared at the well-worn letter she clutched in her hand. She'd read it so often that she'd memorized it, but she still needed to look at the words.

She'd done the right thing, hadn't she?

Dear Signore Stefani,

The Stark Employment Agency forwarded your letter of interest regarding the teaching position. Naturally your skills and experience are well above what I'd hoped for in a piano teacher. It is my privilege to offer you a one-year term of employment. I require only two hours of instruction per day, six days per week. The remaining time would be your own.

Whitethorn Manor is in a very remote part of Cornwall, so if country living is anathema to you the position would not suit.

The letter's author—Mr. Eustace Harrington—went on to offer a generous salary, suggest a start date and give instructions for reaching the manor. Nowhere in the letter did it say Ivo Stefani's *wife* would be an acceptable substitute if the famous pianist was unavailable, uninterested, or . . . dead.

Portia's hands shook as she refolded the brief missive and tucked it into her reticule. It was foolish to submit to her nerves, especially after she'd already accepted the private chaise, the nights in posting inns, and the meals Mr. Harrington's money had provided.

The Music of Love

She groaned and rested her aching temple against the cool glass, exhausted by the relentless whirl of thoughts. Her head had begun to pound several hours earlier and the pain increased with each mile. Weeks and weeks of living with her deception had taken its toll on both her mind and body. Thank God it would soon be over, no matter what happened.

The argument she'd relied on most heavily—that this deception was her only choice—had lost its conviction the closer she came to Whitethorn Manor. But that didn't make it any less true. Portia had no money, no family—at least none who would acknowledge her—and her few friends were almost as poor as she was. She had nothing but debt since she'd been forced to close the Ivo Stefani Academy for Young Ladies.

She laughed and the bitter puff of air left a fleeting fog on the carriage window. Even now the ridiculous name amused her; Ivo had always possessed such grandiose dreams. It was unfortunate his dreams had rarely put food on their table, even before he abandoned her and their struggling school.

Although the small academy had been his idea and bore his name, her husband had pouted whenever Portia asked for help teaching or tutoring.

"Such work is fine for you, *cara*, but my ear bones," he would shudder dramatically at this point, "they are in danger of breaking and bleeding if exposed to such abuse."

"And how will your ear bones feel when they have no place to sleep?" Portia had asked on more than one occasion.

But Ivo had only laughed at her fears—and then run off with a woman whose very existence meant Portia's ten-year marriage was nothing but a sham. Not that any of that mattered now. Ivo was gone and the humiliating truth with him; it no longer signified what he'd done or with whom he'd done it. What mattered was that Portia needed to survive and the only way she could do so was teaching music.

She could have found work in London, but the prospect of starting all over again in the same city had left her feeling tired and hopeless. If she hadn't been destitute she might have considered the offer to share a house with three friends: Serena Lombard, Honoria Keyes, and Lady Winifred Sedgewick, all teachers from her now defunct school.

Unfortunately, all Portia had to offer anyone was debt, and most of it not even hers. But to the dunning agents who dogged her day and night it hadn't mattered that Ivo had generated the mountain of bills without her knowledge.

No, she'd done far better to accept this well-paid position, even though she'd resorted to despicable—and probably criminal—deceit to get it.

The chaise shuddered to a halt and her thoughts scattered like startled pigeons.

Portia peered out the window and caught her breath. It was not a country *house;* it was a mansion: an imposing Palladian-style structure that loomed over the carriage, its massive portico and immense Venetian windows dominating the moonlit sky.

She had arrived.

***

The footmen had just removed their plates when Soames entered the dining room.

"I beg your pardon, sir, it appears the music teacher has arrived."

Stacy Harrington took out his watch. "It's quite late and no doubt he's exhausted after his long journey. I'll wait until morning to speak to him. Show him to his chambers and have Cook send up a tray."

His aged butler did not move.

"Is there something else, Soames?"

"Well . . ."

"Yes, what is it?"

"Well, the thing is, sir, it's *not* Signore Stefani."

Stacy frowned at his usually imperturbable servant. "What is it, Soames?"

"It's *Signora* Stefani," Soames blurted.

"Very well, so he brought his wife with him. I wish he'd let us know, but tonight they can stay in the rooms you have prepared and tomorrow we can move them to a larger apartment."

Soames cleared his throat. "Er, it is *only* Signora Stefani."

His Aunt Frances, who'd been inching closer to the edge of her seat with each new piece of information, could no longer contain herself. "What on earth does he mean, Stacy?" she asked, rattled enough to call him by his childhood pet name in front of a servant.

Stacy didn't mind the slip. In fact, he preferred "Stacy" to "Eustace"—which he'd always thought sounded like an undertaker's name.

He turned from his aunt to his hovering servant. "My aunt wishes to know what on earth you mean, Soames?"

The butler's parchment-like skin flushed. "It appears Signore Stefani is . . . well, he is dead, sir."

His aunt gasped and Stacy sat back in his chair.

"Are you telling me there is a dead body in the carriage, Soames?"

"Oh no, sir, no." Soames stopped and stared a point somewhere beyond Stacy's left shoulder, blinking owlishly. His brow creased and he fingered his long chin. "At least . . ."

"Well?" Stacy prodded when it seemed the ancient man had calcified.

"I understand she is alone in the carriage, sir. No maid or, er, body." He glanced down at his hand. "She brought this with her and claims she is here for the music position."

Soames held out a folded piece of paper and Stacy took it. His own handwriting stared back at him; it was the letter he'd sent Ivo Stefani offering the famous pianist the position. Stacy put the letter aside.

"Very well, show *Signora* Stefani to her room, have Cook send up a tray, and tell *her* I shall speak to her tomorrow."

"Very good, sir."

His aunt waited until the agitated butler left before speaking. "Well."

4

Stacy was amused by how much meaning she put into the single word.

"Well, indeed, Aunt."

"Wouldn't you rather speak to her now? Why wait until morning?"

"She's been in a carriage for almost three days, Aunt Frances. I daresay she is exhausted. Whether I speak to her now or in the morning, she'll still need someplace to spend the night." Besides, the woman had availed herself of a costly journey at his expense; he would question her at his leisure.

"But why has she come, my dear?"

"You heard Soames, Aunt, she's come to teach."

"Was there any mention of this in the correspondence you exchanged?"

"Not a word."

"Can she really expect you to offer her the position after she deceived you?" She stopped, her brow wrinkling. "Unless. . . do you think it possible the hiring agency deceived you?"

"Someone certainly has."

His aunt pursed her lips. "You must send her away."

"I can hardly send her packing in the middle of the night, can I ma'am?"

"I suppose not," she said, grudgingly. "But you must do so first thing tomorrow."

Stacy raised his eyebrows at his aunt's strident tone and she flushed under his silent stare and looked away.

Although his aunt had raised him from infancy, she'd always accepted he was master of both himself and Whitethorn Manor. Stacy couldn't recall the last time she'd told him what he must or mustn't do. She must be far more agitated than she appeared.

He gave her a reassuring smile. "There's nothing to worry about, Aunt Frances. I shall take care of everything in the morning." He took out his watch and glanced at it.

His aunt saw the gesture and stood. "I beg your pardon, my dear, I shall leave you to your port."

The Music of Love

Stacy met her at the dining room door and opened it for her. "I'll join you shortly," he promised before shutting the door behind her.

He extinguished all but one candle and poured himself a larger than average glass of port, taking a sip of the tawny liquid before removing his dark spectacles. The bridge of his nose ached from a day of wearing glasses and he absently massaged it while staring at the dining room ceiling, on which sly cherubs lolled and cavorted on clouds, avidly viewing human folly from a safe distance.

He supposed he should have expected something like this. Not that a woman would show up, of course, but that it would be impossible to engage a musician of Stefani's caliber with such ease. When the employment agency wrote to tell him the famous pianist was seeking a teaching position, Stacy had wondered if it might be some sort of mistake.

Apparently it had been.

He couldn't believe the reputable and well-regarded Stark agency would have lied about Ivo Stefani applying for the position. No, it must have been Mrs. Stefani.

Stacy shook his head. What manner of woman would embark on a long journey under such false pretenses? A bold one? A confident one? A desperate one?

He snorted; certainly a dishonest one.

Stacy could guess *why* she'd deceived him—no doubt she believed he would not engage a woman. He swirled his glass and stared into its warm depths. Would he? His lips twisted at the thought. No, he would not hire a female, although not for the reasons she might suspect.

While men might gawk and stare at him, they tended to overcome their curiosity—eventually. Women, on the other hand . . . Well, let's just say he'd learned the hard way that women were not so forgiving—especially when it came to his eyes.

Stacy could do nothing about their reactions, but he could minimize his exposure to their fear or scorn. Other than his tenants' wives, a few women in the village, and his female servants, he managed to avoid most women. Well, except for the women he visited in Plymouth; those women he generously compensated to ignore his appearance.

It said something about the state of his life that he'd so anticipated the arrival of a music teacher. Perhaps this debacle was a way of telling him his hobby was a foolish waste of time? God knew he had plenty on his plate managing his estates and businesses. But was his life to be devoid of any personal pleasure? He'd already accepted that he could never marry and have a family. Must he also give up playing the piano—one of the few things he loved—just because of his freakish appearance? Was he asking too much to engage a music teacher without fuss and bother? People did it all the time. True, it was usually for their children, but why should that matter?

Stacy put down his glass with more force than necessary, and the crystal clattered on the polished burl wood surface. The more he thought about the woman's deception, the angrier he became. How *dare* this female muck up what was supposed to be a simple business transaction? His aunt had been correct. Stacy should have summoned the woman before him, no matter how exhausted she was, and called her to account for her outrageous deception.

Thinking about his aunt made him realize it had been unkind to send her away when she was only concerned for his welfare—no matter how unnecessary her concern might be. She worried about him as if he were still a little boy rather than a man of five-and-thirty. Frances Tate was his only relative and had been mother and father to him, burying herself in the country and devoting her life to raising him. She'd never been married or even had a beau, as far as Stacy knew. Not for the first time did he feel guilty that she'd built her life around him. Poor Frances, at slightly over six feet tall, she was almost as great a misfit as he was.

Stacy pushed away his glass, picked up his spectacles, and stood. He would make up for his abrupt dismissal by playing for her—that always soothed her.

***

The Music of Love

The butler's reaction to Portia's arrival had been so comical she would have laughed if her future did not hang in the balance. Indeed, if Mr. Harrington's horror was a fraction of his servant's, Portia would have been out in the road with her bags right now— or standing in front of the local magistrate.

Instead, she was in the middle of a luxurious suite comprised of a sitting room, a bedroom, and an enormous dressing room complete with a copper tub. The rooms were airy and spacious and decorated in a soothing combination of icy blue and warm chocolate brown. Portia sank into a wingback chair, took off her sturdy black ankle boots, and stretched her feet on the plush Aubusson carpet. Her body ached, she was dusty and gritty, and her brain was beyond sluggish. Thank God she didn't have to face her prospective employer in this state.

She'd been both stunned and grateful when Mr. Harrington decided to postpone their encounter until morning. Tonight she'd take advantage of her brief reprieve and forget about whatever the master of the house had planned for her; tonight she'd enjoy the luxurious comfort of these rooms.

Portia had just opened her portmanteau and was searching for her nightgown when a maid entered with a large tray of food. The girl gave her a shy smile before carrying the tray to the sitting room and arranging the dishes on a table. She bobbed a curtsey when she'd finished, her large brown eyes brimming with curiosity.

"Mr. Soames said I should help you unpack or ask if you wished for a bath, ma'am."

Portia had the good grace to blush; dinner in her room and an offer of a hot bath? Mr. Harrington was treating her with kindness and courtesy despite her deception.

There was no point unpacking but Portia couldn't turn down a chance to bathe in the beautiful copper tub.

She smiled at the young woman. "I am Signora Stefani. What is your name?"

"Daisy, ma'am."

"I shan't need any help unpacking, Daisy, but I would love a bath after my meal."

"Very good, ma'am." She dropped another curtsey and left, closing the sitting room door behind her.

The smell of food made her mouth water and Portia hastened to examine what the maid had brought: roasted fowl, whipped parsnips, fresh bread and butter, a carafe of wine, and clotted cream with fresh berries. It was the perfect meal for a weary, hungry traveler and she descended on it like a ravenous beast.

She had just popped the last berry into her mouth when Daisy opened the door.

"Your bath is ready, ma'am."

Portia followed her to the copper tub, which was full of steaming water. Beside it was a marble-topped table with a stack of fluffy towels and several crystal decanters.

"Can I help you with your dress, ma'am?"

"Thank you, Daisy, but I shall manage." She waited until the door closed behind the maid before unbuttoning the row of fasteners that ran down the side of her worn, brown traveling costume.

Portia glanced around the room as she undressed. A lovely Chippendale cabinet stood against one wall, rich brown velvet drapes flanked floor-to-ceiling windows, and a massive four-poster bed dominated the bedchamber.

She absently ran a hand over the blue silk counterpane, which felt like a cloud when she pressed her hand into it. A sharp pang shot through her as she considered her surroundings. The housemaid was sweet, the rooms were lovely, and the simple meal had been delicious—what a pity she would most likely have to leave all this tomorrow.

Portia had never received such grand treatment before, not even when she and Ivo had stayed in some of the finest houses in Europe. Her husband had been hailed as a great artist and had been much feted before the accident which had ended his career. Men had paid generous sums to have Ivo Stefani play for their peers,

9

and women had fawned over his olive-skinned good looks and warm bedroom eyes.

But the wife of the great artist had not received the same treatment. For the most part, Portia had stayed in tiny garrets and endured the grudging, slighting treatment of servants while Ivo had bedded the mistress of the house, spent a fortune on expensive frippery, and gambled away most of the money he'd earned.

Portia realized she was gritting her teeth.

Relax, she told herself. *Relax and enjoy the unexpected splendor, because the local magistrate will probably be waiting for you in the morning.*

She pushed away the thought and added a generous splash of lavender-scented bath oil to the steaming water before lowering her tired body into sheer heaven.

By the time she finished washing her hair, her eyelids were heavy with fatigue and she lay back against the warm copper and closed her eyes.

I will rest my eyes. Just for a minute…

Portia woke with a start to cold bathwater, pruned fingers, and pebbled skin. It was all she could do to pull her stiff, aching body from the tub and dry herself. She barely had enough strength left to drag a comb through her damp hair and don her threadbare nightgown before burrowing into the decadent bed. She closed her eyes and was immediately in the grip of a tedious half-dream that revolved around an unending carriage ride.

She was drifting in a deep, dreamless sleep when something awakened her. She pushed aside a tangled mass of curls and squinted at the candle she'd left burning across the room. The clock on her nightstand showed it was just past two.

Portia groaned and dropped her head onto the pillow. In addition to leaving the candle burning, she'd forgotten to draw the curtains, and moonlight flooded the room. She would need to extinguish the candle and close the drapes if she hoped to get any sleep.

Grumbling, she pushed off the blankets, heaved herself out of bed, and padded across the thick carpet to the window. She was about to pull the drapes shut when she noticed a small stone balcony beyond the rippled glass. The well-oiled window latch turned without a sound and she opened the casement and stepped out into a wonderland.

A cool breeze stirred her nightgown and the moon cast a magical glow, illuminating the countryside for miles around. It was one of those moons that hung so low in the sky you felt you could reach out and touch it. Even more light came from a series of lanterns that ran from the corner of the house half-way down the drive.

Portia wondered who would need such a brilliant display of light in the middle of the night but shrugged the thought away. Who knew what country folk did, and why?

Although the night was chilly, it was too beautiful to resist. Portia leaned against the cold stone and filled her lungs with crisp, non-London air, a temporary queen of her moonlit kingdom.

To the west lay a sliver of ocean; the shimmering waves were visible, but too far away to hear them crashing against the shore. Formal gardens surrounded the house to the west and south and beyond them lay a wood large enough to be called a forest.

Portia closed her eyes and drank in the quiet of the night. What a lovely, lovely place this was. And what a terrible shame this would probably be her only night to enjoy it. Her regret was so bitter it left a bad taste in her mouth; she never should have lied. She should've written to Mr. Harrington using her own name. She could've provided him with proof of her training, which was every bit as impressive as Ivo's, not to mention her experience operating a school—not that a closed school was a ringing endorsement.

She'd done them both a disservice by not giving him the truth and allowing him to make his decision. Now her deception would stand between them, and rightly so.

Portia gnawed at her lower lip until it was raw, furious at her impetuosity. She was almost nine-and-twenty, would she never learn to think before she acted? She must have been mad to think this would work, and even if—

The Music of Love

A slight sound intruded on her misery and Portia opened her eyes. Something white and ghostly flickered in the trees at the edge of the woods. She took a step back and stood in the shroud of the heavy velvet drapes, pulling them closer around her body. A figure emerged from the woods and Portia caught her breath as the white blur solidified: It was not a ghost, but a person on a large white horse.

Horse and rider picked their way past the line of trees before exploding into a gallop and blazing across the rolling parkland like a shooting star, closing the distance between the woods and the house in a matter of moments.

The spectral pair slowed as they approached the drive, the bright lanterns affording Portia a better look. No, most certainly not a ghost, but a very substantial-looking man. He wore no coat or waistcoat, only a white shirt that must have become damp from his exertions and now adhered to his torso like a second skin. He controlled his mount with long, muscular thighs encased in breeches and tucked into dark boots. The moonlight turned both horse and man and an eerie silver white.

Portia inched closer to the balcony as he approached, hoping to catch a glimpse of his face as he passed beneath the lantern that hung nearby. The drapes moved with her and the light from the candle behind her escaped and cast a dim line across the cobble drive that was like an arrow pointing toward her window.

Horse and rider swung around as one toward the balcony.

Portia gasped, stumbled back into the room and slammed the casement shut, fumbling with the lock. She pulled the drapes and collapsed against them, her heart pounding as if she'd been running.

Good Lord! How was that possible?

Chapter Two

It was after eleven o'clock by the time a servant arrived to escort Portia to her interview with the master of the house.

She'd been awake, dressed, and waiting for hours—in spite of the fact she'd not had much sleep. She'd tried, but every time she'd closed her eyes a haunting ivory face had flashed into her mind.

And those eyes . . .

Of course she knew it had been a man on the horse and not a ghost or demon. Even so, sleep had evaded her. She'd stared into the darkness above her bed, where phantom images formed and dissolved endlessly.

She'd tried to count sheep or think of other more pleasant things. Like the friends she'd left behind, the five women and one man who'd once been her employees but were now her family. Now her friends were scattered to the four winds, each forced to scratch out an existence on society's fringes. It was probable—likely, in fact—that Portia might never see some of them again.

So here she was; alone, once more.

The thought left her morose, restless, and full of self-pity, and she tossed and turned until the pink fingers of dawn crept over the horizon. Only then had she fallen into a shallow, fitful sleep.

Splinters of bright sunlight penetrated the gap between the velvet drapes and woke her just before eight o'clock. The face that greeted her in the mirror had blood-shot eyes with bags beneath them. Portia wanted to cry when she saw her reflection, but that would have made her nose red, too.

So she'd dressed herself and combed out the frightful mess that was her hair, pulling it back into a knot that was so tight it actually seemed to diminish the bags beneath her eyes.

The Music of Love

And then she'd placed a cool cloth on her forehead and fretted until a knock jarred her from her worries.

It was the butler, Soames.

"Mr. Harrington will see you in the library, ma'am." In contrast to last night, when the old man had appeared almost frantic, this morning his wrinkled face and rheumy blue eyes were the epitome of butleresque impassivity.

They descended a different set of stairs than the one she'd come up the night before. Soames turned right when they reached the bottom and led her down a wide, dimly lit hall before stopping in front of a set of double doors.

He flung open the door on the right and motioned her inside. "The library, ma'am."

Portia peered into the room, the interior of which was hardly visible. The only light came from a single candle on the far side.

"Thank you, Soames." The deep voice came from the same direction as the light. "Please, come in and take a seat, Signora Stefani."

Portia took a hesitant step inside the room and jumped when the door snapped shut behind her.

"I suppose you find it rather dark." A flare of light followed his words and a pale hand lit three more candles. The nimbus of light grew until a skull with two black eye sockets materialized beside it. Portia gasped and the skull shifted into a mask of scorn.

"Please, don't be alarmed. I'm not dangerous and won't harm you."

Her face flamed, both at her foolish reaction and his mocking tone. She could see now that the two black spots were merely dark spectacles and the skull was just a very pale face—the same face she'd seen last night. The moonlight hadn't been playing tricks: Eustace Harrington's hair and skin were as white as freshly fallen snow. Only his frowning lips had any color.

"I have albinism, Signora Stefani. That means I suffer from a lack of pigment. You needn't worry, it's not contagious."

Portia laughed and his expression shifted from scornful to haughty.

"I'm not laughing at you, Mr. Harrington," she hastened to assure him. "I'm laughing because I'm perfectly aware you're not a contagion. I've heard of your condition before." Portia didn't tell him the only other person she'd heard of had been stoned to death by superstitious peasants in a village outside Rome.

"Then I don't have to worry you will faint or scream?" he asked, his tone caustic.

"Not unless you give me good reason to do either, sir."

He ignored her attempt at levity. "Why have you come to Whitethorn Manor?"

Portia took a deep breath and commenced the speech she'd rehearsed all the way from London.

"You wished to engage a music tutor with superior talent—I am such a person. I trained at the Accademia Nazionale di Santa Cecilia, the most respected music school in the world. My father was an instructor there for many years and I was one of his pupils." She paused. When he didn't speak, she continued. "The Accademia doesn't admit women, but I am, nevertheless, a classically trained pianist. I'm not Ivo Stefani, but I'm good. Very good." Portia stopped before her crushing anxiety got the better of her and leaked through her carefully constructed façade.

The white face across from her remained motionless. Had he expected her to apologize? To beg? Something very close to terror spread through her chest, making it difficult to breathe. Perhaps she should—

"When did your husband die?" he asked the question coolly, much as he might ask what time it was or whether she preferred tea to coffee.

Portia swallowed her irritation at his calm, deliberate manner—which made her feel like a recalcitrant schoolgirl standing before a headmistress. She reminded herself that *he* was the injured party in this transaction; she deserved cool treatment, at the very least.

"A little less than a year ago."

"So it was you who responded to my original advertisement and then sent me a letter, signing your husband's name."

Her hot face became even hotter. "Yes."

"If you are so highly qualified, why did you not apply under your own name instead of lying?"

The word *lying* was like a spark on dry tinder.

Portia opened her mouth, but the shrill voice of reason stopped her. *Be humble, Portia! Grovel! Only last night you promised no more impetuous behavior and*—Portia shoved the voice aside. After all—what did she have to lose by speaking her mind? The man was obviously not going to hire her.

"Tell me, Mr. Harrington, would you have engaged a woman tutor?"

He leaned back in his chair, his mouth pulling into a slight smile. "That's hardly the point, is it?"

The man was toying with her and feeding off her humiliation and fear. She shot to her feet and he stood with her.

"Are you leaving, Signora Stefani?"

"Why should I stay? You've made your opinion of female musicians quite clear."

"Oh? I thought we were speaking of your deception rather than your musical abilities."

Portia ground her teeth, furious that he was correct. Again.

He gestured to her chair. "Please, won't you be seated? I've gone to a great deal of effort and expense to bring you here. Won't you extend me the courtesy of a few minutes of your time and perhaps some answers?"

Everything he said was fair—maddeningly so—but for some reason that did nothing to mollify her unreasonable anger.

"And what will you do if I refuse, Mr. Harrington? Summon the local magistrate?"

He sighed. "I *am* the local magistrate, Signora Stefani."

Portia gave a short, mirthless laugh and dropped into her chair. "Ask whatever you like."

He resumed his seat, ignoring both her rude behavior and angry words. "I'm curious why there was no mention of your husband's death in the papers, Signora?"

She'd expected this question much sooner, but that didn't mean she was eager to begin telling even more lies.

"My husband did not die in England." She paused, "Perhaps you heard of his accident?"

"Yes, his arm was badly crushed and he could no longer play. I assumed that was why he responded to my advertisement."

"I'm afraid my husband found teaching an unbearable reminder of everything he'd lost." That much was true. "He needed to get away from the memories of his past and do something meaningful with his life. He decided the best way to do that was to join the army." *Lies, lies, lies.* Luckily her face couldn't get any hotter.

Pale eyebrows shot up above his dark glasses, a reaction that could mean surprise, disbelief, or some other emotion. Portia assumed it was surprise. After all, he hadn't known Ivo. If he had, he'd be doubled over with laughter right now: Ivo Stefani had not entertained an altruistic thought in his entire life.

"Please continue."

"There's not much more to tell. He went to Naples and died shortly afterward in the Battle of Tolentino." Would he dare to ask which side her husband fought with? Or would he assume the worst and dismiss her on the spot for being the widow of a man some in England might consider a traitor?

"Tell me, Signora," he said, resting his elbows on his desk and leaning forward, the action bringing his fascinating face closer to the light. "What did you think would happen when you presented yourself to me under false pretenses?"

She'd asked herself the same thing—but in more brutal words—countless times. Why, then, was she so angry when he asked her a question he had every right to ask?

Because you're ashamed of what you've done and nothing is more agonizing than knowing one is in the wrong.

The annoying little voice was correct, but that didn't mean Portia had to like it. Still, she *could* control her behavior better.

"I'm sorry for my deception and I apologize." She clamped her lips shut. But then her mouth opened and more words tumbled out. "If you tell me what you spent to bring me here, I will gladly repay you." She stunned herself with the foolish words; just where would she get the money?

Pride goeth before destruction, and a haughty spirit before a fall.

Portia ground her teeth at the smug, but apt, observation.

Mr. Harrington's features shifted into an expression of mild distaste. "We could haggle like costermongers over repayment for your journey or you could give me a demonstration of your musical ability." His pale lips twisted into a mocking smile. "I know which I would prefer."

Portia bristled at his sarcasm but hope surged in her breast. Would he consider engaging her? Or was this some petty form of revenge?

She studied his unreadable face. He reminded her of the famous stone she'd seen in the British Museum—the one named after the Egyptian port city of Rosetta. He bore no *physical* resemblance to the black chunk of rock, but he emanated the same inscrutable quality. Was he toying with her? Raising her hopes just so he could—

Portia seized control of her whirling thoughts. The truth was, she didn't care *what* his motivations were. Playing the piano was far better than answering questions for which she had no answers or at least none that were palatable.

She inclined her head with hauteur to match his. "You are entitled to a demonstration of my abilities. What would you like me to play?"

"I will leave that to your discretion. You are, after all, the expert," he added wryly. "Shall I take you to the music room right now or do you need time to prepare?"

Portia heard the challenge beneath his taunting question and smiled; what a pleasure it would be to shove his scornful words down his throat. She stood. "There is no time like the present, Mr. Harrington."

Chapter Three

Portia stole glances at Eustace Harrington as he led her down the long hall. His aquiline nose, shapely lips, and chiseled jaw were the stuff of classical sculpture and his skin and fashionably cut hair were whiter even than alabaster. Only his glasses disturbed the vision of a male version of Galatea come to life: Eustace Harrington was the most fascinating-looking man she'd ever seen.

He opened the door to a room every bit as dark as the library and turned to her, a Sphinx-like smile curving his lips. "Pardon my rudeness Signora, but I'm going to precede you and light the way." He lit five candles in the candelabrum beside the piano before taking a seat as far from the light as possible, effectively hiding himself from her view.

Portia approached the instrument and stopped abruptly. "My goodness."

"What is it, Signora?"

"You have a Schmidt." She ran her fingers reverently across the glossy case.

"You approve?" His voice held the first hint of warmth she'd heard.

"It's a piano worthy of a concert dais." Even Ivo had never played on finer.

"There is sheet music in the cabinet behind you."

It was Portia's turn to smile mockingly. "That won't be necessary." She seated herself and ran through a few scales to loosen her hands. The instrument was easily the finest she'd ever played. The pianos her father had used to teach his students had been well-made, but most of them had been abused by hundreds

19

of hands and years of constant use. This piano was exquisite, the sound immaculate.

She launched into Bach's Goldberg Variations, beginning with "Variatio 14. a 2 Clav."

The piece was lively—almost giddy—and the multitude of cross-overs was a perfect way to demonstrate her technical ability for the man who sat in judgment of her.

Portia could claim, without exaggeration, that she'd been Ivo's superior when it came to Bach.

"Of course you favor him," Ivo had taunted her in a fit of pique. "He has no passion, only mathematics—perfect for your English soul." He'd often flung the fact she was half-English at her as if that were some sort of flaw.

Portia moved without pause to "Variatio 15. Canone alla Quinta. a 1 Clav.: Andante." It was sheer pain and coiled itself around her and squeezed and squeezed, leaving her battered and bruised by the time she moved to the last selection.

"Variatio 5" was sweetness and light and it washed over her like a healing rain, soothing her with its gentle, caressing tranquility.

When the final notes left her fingers, Portia folded her hands in her lap and looked into the darkness. A long pause followed, which was something Mr. Harrington appeared to excel at.

"Your playing is exquisite." An almost undetectable tremor ran beneath his cool voice and Portia didn't bother to hide her triumphant smile. Good! Bach should never leave a person unmoved.

"It appears your claims were not hyperbole, you are a very good musician."

Portia refused to acknowledge such faint praise; she was beyond good.

"I was going to suggest a trial period to see if we might suit . . ." his words trailed off, as if he'd surprised himself with the offer. He'd certainly surprised Portia—rendered her dumbstruck, in fact. "But since you appear to have taken me in dislike—"

"I would be honored," Portia blurted before he could retract his offer. "And very grateful." She squirmed in the agonizing pause that followed. The distant ticking of a clock was the only sound and Portia was just about to start babbling when his cool, unhurried voice pierced the darkness between them.

"I think a month would be sufficient. At the end of the trial period I will either extend an offer for the full term of employment or I will pay you for the month and arrange for your journey back to London."

Portia's pride rebelled at the not-so-subtle threat behind his words: She'd better perform to his liking if she wanted to stay.

Fortunately, this time she seized control of her pride, wrestled it into submission, and swallowed her irrational temper. "That sounds more than fair, Mr. Harrington." She hesitated, "A month will give me time to see if I like living in such a remote location."

He chuckled at her small show of defiance, the sound warm and inviting and at odds with his chilly manner and remote exterior. "You've never lived in the country before, Signora?"

"I've done little more than drive *through* the countryside."

"Ah. Well, I should hate to keep you here now that you've seen how rural we are. Perhaps you would rather return to London?"

Portia almost laughed; the clever snake had let her tie her own noose and then insert her neck. It was too bad for him she refused to hang herself.

"I've come a long way, Mr. Harrington. It would be foolish not to give the situation a chance." Her stomach churned in the taut silence that followed.

"How shall you structure my lessons, Signora Stefani?"

Dizzying relief washed through her body and Portia scrambled to gather her wits. "I will need to determine your level of skill to answer that question. Is there a time of day you prefer to play?"

"I usually practice a few hours before dinner."

"Let us keep to your schedule. Today you can play whatever you've been working on, which will give me a chance to assess your strengths and weaknesses."

21

He emerged from the gloom and stopped short of the candelabrum. "I am less prone to eye strain if the light is dim. Will that be an issue?" He used one long, elegant finger to push his black spectacles up the bridge of his equally elegant nose.

Portia wrenched her eyes away from his mesmerizing face and stared at his stylish cravat instead. "As long as you are able to see the notes on the page," she said lightly.

"Then I shall meet you here at four o'clock. That will leave you with two hours to rest before dinner. My aunt and I take our midday meals separately but meet for dinner. We dine at eight o'clock, which is rather late for the country. You will, of course, join us."

Portia flushed at the unexpected offer—although it was really more of a command—thrilled she wouldn't be banished to her room for the next month.

"I would be delighted."

"Do you ride, Signora?"

"I'm afraid riding was not part of growing up in Rome. I am fond of walking, however, and the countryside looks lovely."

"We have our share of walking paths," he agreed, "but a gig will allow you to access town more readily. I will instruct Hawkins, my stable master, to show you how to operate the conveyance."

"That is most kind of you."

Harrington inclined his head. "I shall see you at four, Signora."

Portia waited until he'd turned before closing her eyes, weak with relief. She could stay—at least for now—and wouldn't have to beg and scrape her way back to London and live off her friends' charity.

"One more thing Signora."

Portia looked up and saw her new employer was standing in the open doorway.

"Yes, Mr. Harrington?"

"As far as I'm concerned the subject of your deception is closed. I will not bring it up again."

She smiled. "Thank you."

22

"However, I want you to understand I do not tolerate lying from the people I employ."

His cool rebuke crushed the gratitude Portia had been feeling and her hackles rose. But she triumphed over her nature and caught the angry retort before it left her mouth.

"I understand, Mr. Harrington."

He nodded and the door clicked shut behind him.

Portia stared into the dimness, the exhilaration of only a few moments ago now tainted by anger—and fear. His words echoed in her head and she ruthlessly pushed them to the back of her mind. She'd told him everything he *needed* to know. The truth about her past was none of his concern and made no difference to her teaching. All Mr. Harrington needed to know about her life with Ivo was that he was gone.

***

Stacy sat down at his desk, extinguished the candles, and removed his glasses, letting his eyes rest in the velvety blackness of the library.

What the bloody hell had he just done? He'd gone in there determined to give her a proper raking and send her packing; instead, he'd been stupefied by her playing and then offered her a damned job.

He was *still* awed by her brief performance—a masterful demonstration of passion and precision he could never aspire to.

Don't forget her person, a sly voice in his head reminded him.

Stacy snorted. As if that were bloody likely.

He'd caught only a glimpse of her last night, but it had been enough to pique his interest. She'd looked wild on the balcony, her eyes huge, her full lips forming a surprised *O* when he'd caught her spying. Untamed spirals of dark hair haloed her pale face, her thin garment rendered all but transparent by the candlelight behind her.

Blood rushed to his groin at the memory of her voluptuous silhouette.

Christ. Stacy shifted in his chair.

The Music of Love

Last night's woman had been alluring, but so had this morning's, although for entirely different reasons.

Gone were the wild eyes and in their place was a haughty stare. She'd restrained her magnificent hair so brutally Stacy wondered if he'd only imagined her unruly curls. Her serviceable brown dress was high-necked and long sleeved, but it could not hide the enticing body he'd so briefly seen last night.

Her nose, undoubtedly a gift from some Italian ancestor, was her most prominent feature and ensured she'd never be considered a conventional beauty. That said, her dusky hair, creamy skin, and voluptuous body made for a delicious—and dangerous—combination.

But her attractive person wasn't all that captured his interest.

She'd entered the library prepared for battle, armed only with her pride and talent—but, oh, what formidable weapons those turned out to be!

A fire burned inside her and Stacy had seen the flames—hell, he'd been scorched by them—when she spoke of her ability. She'd faced him with an arrogant confidence that had been damn near erotic, and, as it turned out, not at all unwarranted.

And then he'd become aroused when she'd played.

He should be ashamed by his body's earthy reaction, but he wasn't. A man would have to be dead from the neck down *not* to become hard. She'd swung from tightly laced to tempestuous and flushed—like a woman in the throes of passion—in the blink of an eye. The experience had not only been arousing, it had been soul-shattering: Stacy could practice for a hundred years and never play half as well.

But that didn't mean he couldn't *try*.

There was no doubt in his mind Signora Stefani had much to teach him—but would he be able to learn anything in her distracting presence?

You are not some rutting buck sensing a mate. Surely you can control your urges?

Of course he could control his urges, but control or lack of it was not the bloody question. The question was: Would he be able to concentrate on his music or would he spend his lessons fantasizing about bending her over the piano?

Stacy grimaced. It sounded more than a little pathetic when put so baldly.

But the truth *was* pathetic: He was randy. Terribly randy, in fact. He'd spent most of the last two months in Barnstaple, busy with the refitting of two new ships. As a result, it had been ages since his last visit to the Plymouth establishment where he satisfied such urges.

Ha! Establishment?

Fine. The brothel I frequent. Is that better?

Stacy refused to be ashamed of what he did. Paying a prostitute was a far better practice than getting bastards on one's servants or local maidens, a thing the local squire did with disgusting frequency.

There is always a wife.

He didn't even bother to justify that ridiculous thought.

The truth was that he should've set up a mistress long ago, but the notion left him cold. What a lot of bother not only for him, but also for some poor woman. What must it be like to sit around one's house all day waiting for a man to arrive and mount you?

Thoughts of mounting made his body tighten and he dropped his head against the back of his chair. A month was a bloody long time and he was already lusting after the poor widow, a woman who was only here to earn her bread.

Stacy frowned, sobered by that thought. He'd always been sickened by men who preyed on their tenants, servants, or other dependents. So, all he needed to do for the next thirty days was think of Signora Stefani as just another servant. Just a month, and then he would do what he should have done this morning and send her away. Surely he could suppress his unseemly urges for a month?

The Music of Love

"Hell," he muttered, squeezing his temples, it was going to be a long month.

THANKS FOR READING!

Keep reading for a sneak peek of MELISSA AND THE VICAR:

Chapter One

Melissa Griffin stared into red eyes that burned with malevolence.

Her breath froze in her chest but her heart made up for her lungs' mutiny by thundering in her ears. She took a minute step back, but her tormentor strode inexorably closer. She shuffled to the side, but he followed her sideways, too.

"What do you want from me?" She forced the words through gritted teeth.

The foul, evil beast said nothing, stalking ever closer.

There were only two choices: she could run or she could fight—and there was no chance she would vanquish such an implacable foe.

Mel silently counted to three, grabbed two fistfuls of her skirts, and broke into a run while screaming, "*Heeeeelp!*"

She flew past a tiny daub and wattle cottage that looked like it should have housed angels instead of this nasty brute. Something struck the back of one leg and Mel risked a glimpse at her pursuer: he was right behind her, dogged and menacing and—

"Ooof!" Melissa slammed into a wall that was hard and warm and . . . human.

The human wall grunted. "Here, then, don't be afraid," a deep voice soothed.

Mel was blind to everything except the red eyes and razor-sharp claws behind her and plowed through the thicket of limbs, climbing the stranger's body as if he were a tree.

Melissa and the Vicar

Strong arms slid around her, lifted her, and spun her around before depositing her on the ground, his body a shield—a substantial one, at that—between Melissa and that *fiend.*

"Hector!" Her protector's deep voice was overlaid with a tone of command that demanded to be obeyed.

When only silence met his order, Mel stood on her toes and peeked over broad, black-clad shoulders, pale blond hair tickling her nose.

Her jaw dropped at what she saw: the demon had screeched to a halt and was ambling away in the opposite direction, behaving as if butter wouldn't melt in his mouth, er, beak.

"Why that—that—"

"Rooster?" the same deep voice said, this time laced with amusement rather than command.

Mel realized she'd pasted the front of her body to the back of his and took a hasty step back. He turned and she blinked; it might have been the conceit of a city dweller, but she'd not expected to see a man as lovely as her savior in the middle of a country lane. In fact, Melissa could not recall seeing a man as beautiful—yes, beautiful—as this one *ever.* And he was wearing a clerical collar.

"I've been rescued from that—that *hellion* by a vicar?"

Rather than be insulted by her disbelieving tone he smiled, a warm, charming, gorgeous smile that should not have belonged to a man of the cloth. Not that she knew anything whatsoever about vicars and what type of smiles they should or did have. Men of the cloth tended to be thin on the ground in her line of business. For all she knew, *all* clergymen were this attractive. Perhaps it was a prerequisite of the job? Was that how they filled their pews on Sunday?

"I'm afraid I don't have the honor of being a vicar—yet. So things are even worse, you see: you've actually been rescued by a mere curate." He executed a graceful bow. "Mister Stanwyck at your service, Miss. . ."

Melissa pulled her gaze away from his mouth, which definitely was wasted on a vicar, and said, "Er, Griffin."

"A pleasure, Miss Griffin."

His eyes were the clear, guileless blue of the sky and they met her own rather than roaming her body. Mel's inner critic—as vociferous and relentless as a Greek choir—pointed out that not every man in Great

Britain wished to lay themselves out at her feet. Even if it *had* seemed that way since she'd been fourteen.

"I know everyone in New Bickford so you must be a visitor, Miss Griffin."

"Yes. I—I've come to the country to convalesce."

His brow furrowed and his expression shifted to one of genuine sympathy. "I am sorry to hear you've been ill." He wasn't just mouthing a platitude; he actually *sounded* sorry.

"I am on the mend now, just—"

"Mister Stanwyck! Yoohoo!" The voice floated toward them from the direction of the quaint little cottage which the vile Hector apparently called home. Right now said villain was placidly scratching among his hen harem, pausing a moment here and there to execute what must have been some type of hen-attracting side-step shuffle, his chest puffed out.

Melissa glared at him; how *dare* he look so harmless?

The curate greeted the approaching woman. "Hello, Miss Philpot. And how are you this afternoon?"

The woman in question was a tall, gangly female easily twice the curate's age who was sporting a coquettish smile and the eyelash batting airs of a schoolroom miss.

"Oh, Mr. Stanwyck, Gloria will be so relieved you are here." Her bulbous green orbs swiveled toward Melissa and her steel gray eyebrows dropped like twin guillotines. "And you've brought. . .your sister?" The last word was spoken in such a hopeful tone that Melissa had to bite her lip to keep from laughing.

The curate pressed his too-beautiful lips together in a mild smile that was belied by the twinkle in his eyes. "I'm afraid my parents did not see fit to bless me with any sisters, ma'am, only brothers."

Miss Philpot was nothing if not adaptable. She turned from Mel, her expression softening as she gazed at the curate. "Well that is certainly the lord's work if they are all as handsome and sweet-natured as *you*, Mr. Stanwyck."

The curate accepted the compliment with a smile and gestured to Melissa. "This is Miss Griffin. I'm afraid she just had a—well, I don't suppose you would call it a run-*in* so much as a run-*away*, with Hector."

Mel narrowed her eyes at his witticism and was rewarded by one of his stunning smiles.

Melissa and the Vicar

Miss Philpot wagged an admonishing finger at the vicious animal. "Oh, Hector! Have you been over-vigilant?" She spoke in a tolerant, cooing tone that sent Hector into another of his sideways step-slides. Miss Philpot tittered appreciatively at the maneuver. It seemed the bird's debatable charms worked on more than just his hens; maybe Hector was smarter than he looked.

Miss Philpot turned to Mel. "I *do* apologize for Hector's enthusiasm, Miss, er, Griffin." The affection in her eyes—a residual product of Hector's charm—slid away to reveal a zealous gleam that would have done a Spanish Inquisitor proud. "Are you just visiting our village on your way to . . . somewhere else?"

Miss Philpot wasn't the only one waiting for her response with interest. The cerulean blue eyes of the curate were also turned her way.

Something about his clear gaze made Mel shy and fidgety, a feeling she'd not had since selling oranges on street corners when she was a girl. She brushed off the skirt of her walking costume, as though Hector might have been pelting her with rotted fruits and vegetables rather than just his—she paused to eye the rooster, and was forced to admit, *very* scrawny—body.

"I am staying in a house down the way." She gestured with the hand that wasn't clutching her reticule and then realized she'd motioned in the direction of the ocean. Both members of her small audience wore slight frowns of confusion. Melissa bestowed her most winning smile on Miss Philpot, curious to see if it had any effect on the woman. It did not.

"I'm sorry, I'm afraid I'm a bit turned around." She pointed toward the path she'd just sprinted down a few moments earlier. "I am staying at Halliburton Manor."

Miss Philpot's eyes widened. "Halliburton Manor?"

"Yes, that is correct." Why was the woman looking at her that way?

"Ah . . . I see. How unusual that we heard nothing about it."

Mel wondered if she was supposed to place an announcement in the local newspaper or contact the town crier. "I expect that is because I dealt with an agent in London and brought all my own servants."

"Ah. And you are staying there, er, alone?"

Melissa suppressed a twinge of annoyance at the prying questions; this was the sort of curiosity she should have expected when coming to such a small village. "I—"

4

"Mister Stanwyck!" a voice trilled from the direction of the cottage. "How delightful to see you. But Agnes, why are you keeping the reverend standing out—oh," the newcomer said when she noticed Melissa. "I'm so sorry. I didn't see you there."

"Gloria, this is the new tenant in Halliburton Manor—Miss Griffin. Miss Griffin, my sister, Miss Gloria Philpot."

Mel would have known without being told this was Miss Philpot's sister since the two women were mirror images of each other.

"Halliburton Manor?" Miss Gloria aimed a curious expression Melissa's way. Just what was it about her choice of residence that was so interesting?

Miss Gloria opened her mouth, no doubt to take over the inquisition, but the curate took charge of the conversation. "You must be walking to town, Miss Griffin? Perhaps I might show you the way?"

Mel thought he looked . . . hopeful.

The Misses Philpot, on the other hand, looked forlorn.

"But, Mr. Stanwyck, didn't you just come *from* town? Won't you come in for some tea?" The elder Miss Philpot stared accusingly at Melissa while she spoke, as if Mel were some sort of siren leading the curate toward jagged rocks.

"And I thought you were going to look at our wisteria trellis, the bit that needs mending," Miss Gloria added when the curate didn't jump on the offer of tea.

Mel couldn't help herself. "Yes, Mister Stanwyck. I should *hate* to deprive you of tea. And the trellis."

A muscle at the corner of his shapely mouth twitched. "I'll just walk Miss Griffin into the village—and show her the church along the way—and be back in half a jiffy. Not to worry, I shall see to the trellis before the day is out." His hand was at her elbow and he'd managed to turn them both and start down the path without Mel even realizing it.

"Goodbye, ladies. It was a pleasure to meet you," she tossed over her shoulder at the frowning women. She turned to the reverend, who was walking briskly, as if to put some distance between himself and the two disappointed members of his flock. "A *half* a jiffy, Mr. Stanwyck? I don't believe I've heard that particular expression before."

He chuckled, his hand falling away from her arm. "Why do I feel that you enjoy a bit of mischief-making, Miss Griffin?"

Melissa and the Vicar

"I certainly don't *run away* from mischief—not like I run from nasty little feathered, beaked goblins."

He made a *tsking* sound. "I can see you're going to hold that slip of the tongue against me, aren't you?"

"Perhaps."

He cut her a look of mock severity. "To err is human but to forgive is divine, Miss Griffin."

"I'm afraid I'm far more familiar with erring, Mr. Stanwyck." He had no idea just how true that was.

"Hmm, I *see*. Well, I must warn you that Hector is something of a favorite in these parts. It would cast a shadow over your reputation to be heard bandying about such opprobrium regarding his character or, er, stature."

Mel laughed. "Well, I wouldn't want to have a shadowy reputation."

"Indeed." He grinned down at her, looking like the least probable example of a clergyman in all of Britain. "Now, I'm afraid we departed before Miss Philpot could winkle out all your pertinent details."

"Winkle away, Reverend."

"When did you arrive at Halliburton Manor, Miss Griffin?"

"Just yesterday."

"Ah, that explains why neither of the Misses Philpot knew of your arrival. They are early to bed—with the chickens, as it were."

Mel cast him a sideways look and then wished she hadn't. With his striking white-blond hair, huge blue eyes—fringed with dark, rather than blond, lashes of course—and classical features, he really was a gorgeous specimen of manhood and that *was* an area which she could claim expertise. Although he resembled an angel, he was as solidly muscled as a bull beneath his loose-fitting suit—she knew that from having his arms tight around her.

The fact that he was dressed in the sober attire of a clergyman somehow made his fair good looks even more appealing. Or perhaps that was just the novelty of him?

While Melissa was more knowledgeable about men than she cared to be, she'd rarely associated with the wholesome type and she'd *never* spoken to a member of the clergy—at least not that she was aware of. Something about walking beside him made her feel. . . anxious. Most likely it was just that he did not fit neatly into any of her categories of men. Or perhaps it was because she thought God might strike her down

6

at any moment for having the audacity to associate with one of his Chosen Ones.

"Have a care, Miss Griffin." A strong, steadying hand reappeared at her elbow and he steered her around a prominent tree root in the path.

"Thank you." She'd do better to pay more attention to where she was going and less to inventorying the man beside her.

"Do you have an appointment in town or can you take a moment to come and see our fine church windows?" he asked after they'd walked a moment in silence.

She had nothing *but* time. But did she really want to go inside a church? After all, it hadn't been her intention to actually attend services or even interact with any of the villagers. That had been the point of leasing a house *outside* of town.

"Our windows are considered some of the finest in this part of England," he added, the humor in his voice making her risk another glance. Lord! His eyes were *sparkling* at her. Were curates supposed to sparkle? Surely not.

"Well, I can't say no to that, can I?" Mel asked, her tone tarter than she'd intended. "But I cannot stay long because I'm to meet up with my aunt."

"I'll show you only the high points and that way deliver you to your aunt in good time."

"Oh, you needn't deliver me to her, I'll be—"

"I can introduce you to the vicar, Mr. Heeley, if he is about."

"No, really, you needn't go out of your way." Lord, the last thing she needed was to meet more clergy. It would be a miracle if she didn't turn to a pillar of salt, or smoke, or stone, or suffer some sort of divine punishment, not that she'd ever actually *read* any of the Bible or had any idea of what type of punishment was meted out between its covers.

"It would be my pleasure," he said, interrupting her muddled thoughts, but not before she realized that she *wanted* to see his windows and be delivered to the village by him. When was the last time a man had cared enough about her safety to deliver her anywhere? Well, a man other than her dear friend Joss, of course. Perhaps it might be nice to receive such care? That realization only served to annoy her; she had most certainly *not* come to the country to engage in casual flirtation—especially not with a bloody vicar.

Melissa and the Vicar

"Is giving every visitor to New Bickford a personal tour part of your strenuous curate's duties?"

"Oh yes. I'm responsible for any number of things: taking tea with parishioners, mending trellises, showing off church windows, rescuing damsels in distress from feathered predators—Ah, here we are, to the left if you would, Miss Griffin." He gestured toward an ornate gate set in an old stone wall. "This is the back way into the churchyard now, but it used to be the original lychgate." He lifted the heavy horseshoe-shaped latch and pushed open the gate. "It is a rare example of the Gothic style." He waited until she'd gone through and closed it behind her. "Back in those days they called this a *resurrection gate*."

Melissa noticed they'd stepped into a graveyard filled with worn, tilted headstones. "Why is this gate no longer used?" She frowned, "Actually, just what is a lychgate *for*?"

He gestured to the heavy beams topping the gate. "It was a place to shelter the coffin before burial, hence the gate's unusual substance. The path we just came down is what people used to call a *corpse road*."

Mel shivered.

"Are you chilled, Miss Griffin?" He wore a look of concern but she saw the humor lurking in his eyes.

"No, that was merely a case of the shivers, which is exactly what you expected after telling me such a gruesome piece of information." She raised an eyebrow at him. "Confess it, Mister Stanwyck—you *wanted* to give me the shivers."

He laughed, his even white teeth adding to his list of perfections. "You'll have to forgive me; I have so few amusements."

Somehow Mel doubted that.

"It is at this point in my tour where I point out our magnificent spire." He leaned low and close, as if to view something from her height and perspective, and then held out his arm and pointed. "Can you see just the tip of it above that big chestnut tree?"

Melissa was conscious of the heat of his body and his clean, masculine scent. She ignored her body's unwanted twinge of interest and followed the direction of his pointing finger, to where a foot of gray stone was visible above the tree canopy.

"The church and the gate were built together?" she asked, aware of the pulse beating at the base of her throat and glad when he stood and put some distance between their bodies.

"You have an excellent eye for architecture, Miss Griffin."

"Now you are guilty of flattery, Mr. Stanwyck."

He gave the same warm chuckle as before and Melissa decided eliciting such a velvety laugh could prove an enjoyable pastime. Before she could give that alarming thought the scrutiny it deserved, another man dressed in the clothing of a clergyman came toward them.

"Ah, Mr. Stanwyck. Good morning."

"I was hoping our paths would cross, Vicar. Mr. Heeley, may I introduce Miss Griffin? She is new to our area and has just taken up residence at Halliburton Manor."

The vicar, a bone-thin man who looked to be in his late sixties or early seventies, stiffened at something his curate said, his reaction not dissimilar to the Philpots'. But he recovered quickly and turned his deep-set gray eyes on her. His mouth curved into a warm smile. "Welcome to New Bickford, Miss Griffin. I am very glad to hear that Halliburton Manor has a tenant again."

"Thank you, Mr. Heeley."

"I encountered Miss Griffin not far from the Philpot cottage. She was, er, finding it difficult to pass."

The vicar chuckled. "Ah, Hector, was it?" He nodded at his own question, not appearing to need an answer. "He is a fierce protector who is cast in the mold of the ancients. A most excellent rooster."

The curate gave her a look that said, *See, I told you so.*

Mel's lips parted.

"Indeed, you speak the truth, Vicar," Mister Stanwyck interjected when Melissa couldn't quite find the words she was looking for to express her thoughts on Hector. He cut her a sideways glance and rocked back on his heels. "Hector is one of the Titans."

"And how long will you stay with us, Miss Griffin?" the vicar asked, pulling her away from the narrow-eyed look she was giving the teasing curate.

It was time to share the story she'd concocted. "Until the end of the summer." She cleared her throat. "I was ill last winter and have come to the country with my aunt to partake of the country air."

"Ah, I see. You are from the city?"

"Yes, we are both from London."

"Well," the vicar said, his tone brisk as he rubbed his hands together, as if he'd just completed a task and was brushing away the remnants. "I know I'm biased, but I believe there is no town in Great Britain better than ours for peace and healing. We are a close community but also one which respects the privacy of our members."

Melissa hoped he was correct. Because anyone who pried too deeply into her story would find something they wouldn't care to discover.

"Well, I shall leave you and Mr. Stanwyck to continue your tour. It was a pleasure, Miss Griffin, and I shall see you on Sunday."

Melissa made some non-committal sound, waiting until the vicar was out of earshot before turning to the curate.

"I can't help but think people are surprised to hear I'm staying at Halliburton Manor?"

His cheekbones—high, sharp, and beautiful—looked even more appealing with a faint red stain. "I'm afraid the last inhabitant, er, well, she met a rather tragic end."

Mel dipped her chin when he stopped. "Yes?"

"She was a widow. Her husband was—" he grimaced. "Well, he was killed in a military engagement in India. Mrs. Symes took her own life."

It was a sad story, of course, but she still didn't see—

"Mrs. Symes had not seen her husband for eleven months." He hesitated and said, "She was with child when she died."

Ahh, now she understood the odd looks. And the reason for them made her fume.

"I see—a tragedy *and* a scandal." She cut him an arch look that was not playful. "Or do the good and proper villagers even see it as a tragedy?"

He blinked in surprise. "Death is always a tragedy, Miss Griffin." It was an answer, but not one to the question she had asked. He leaned toward her, his blue eyes shadowed with concern. "You look flushed. I believe I've tired you out dragging you about."

She swallowed her irritation at the story he'd told. She'd known something was going on when the two older women, the Philpots, had assumed that faint, virtuous air. Melissa had been the recipient of that look more times than she could count.

Take hold of yourself, Mel!

Yes, she'd better. After all, she'd known a small community often meant small mindedness, but she'd come here, anyway.

You came here to rest and make some important decisions, not to battle rural prejudice.

10

She forced herself to smile. "Thank you for your concern, but I'm fine. I am, however going to be late so perhaps I'd better be on my way. Maybe you can show me the church some other day." Though not if she had any say about it.

No, the story he'd just told her made it painfully clear she didn't need to make friends here—in fact, that was a terrible idea. And making friends with a man of the cloth—especially this handsome, kind, and curious curate? Well, that was the worst thing she could do. For both of them.

Chapter Two

Magnus's clerical collar felt oddly stiff and scratched his neck as he watched Miss Griffin walk away down New Bickford's narrow main street—its only street, really—with her aunt, Mrs. Daisy Trent.

Mrs. Trent had been waiting for her niece at New Bickford's tiny inn, the Sleeping Ferret, enjoying a pot of tea in their private parlor.

And what an aunt Mrs. Trent was. Certainly nothing like any of Magnus's numerous aunts, none of whom were tall, buxom, and bold eyed. He also suspected Mrs. Trent was wearing cosmetics, although he wasn't familiar enough with such things to be certain.

The two women looked nothing alike. Miss Griffin was a delicate, pale, almost ethereally beautiful auburn-haired goddess who appeared too fragile for this world. Her aunt, on the other hand, epitomized earthiness. Not just her lush body, but her full smiling lips and the knowing glint in her eyes. Magnus had felt as if she were inspecting his person and stripping away his clothing in the process. It was a strange feeling and he'd no doubt imagined it.

After the women had taken their leave from Magnus they'd disappeared into Cooper's Mercantile together. It hadn't been his plan linger outside the shop and spy on the two newest members of New Bickford through the diamond-paned windows, but neither was he in a hurry to get away.

Magnus was re-living his brief conversation with the delectable Miss Griffin when a voice behind him pulled him out of his pleasant musing.

"Mr. Stanwyck—a word, please."

He turned to find Mrs. Pilkington and her three daughters approaching him and bit back a groan.

"Ah, good afternoon, ma'am."

If you asked anyone who knew Magnus even a little bit whether he was arrogant, proud, or conceited, they would have thrown back their head and laughed. It was true: he wasn't proud about his physical appearance, which he viewed as a product of two attractive parents, rather than any efforts on his part.

He'd never aspired to be a pink of the *ton* and his clothing—even before he'd entered the clergy—had always been functional and comfortable rather than stylish. His only real contribution to his outward appearance was to keep his body healthy and fit, which happily was an unexpected byproduct of being an active country curate.

Just because Magnus wasn't conceited about his looks didn't mean he was insensible to their effect on the feminine sex. It hadn't taken him long to realize that excessive interest in his person was an inconvenience for a curate who was not in a position to marry.

It wasn't his ability to resist all the lures that were tossed his way that worried him. Rather, it was the sheer exhaustion he experienced from having to fight so many silent, relentless skirmishes.

Like Mrs. Pilkington and her three daughters, for example.

"Mister Stanwyck," Mrs. Pilkington said in her strident voice while her daughters spread out around him. The eldest Miss Pilkington moved into position on his left flank, her middle sister on his right, and the youngest drifted somewhere behind him—a maneuver they must have learned from studying a tactical map of Hannibal's movements at the Battle of Cannae.

Magnus took pride in meeting his opponent head on and without flinching. "Good afternoon, Mrs. Pilkington." He turned slightly and nodded to the girls. "Ladies."

"I have not received your response to our Summer Soiree invitation yet, Mr. Stanwyck."

Ah, yes, the blasted soiree.

Magnus had begun to suspect that *soiree* was another word for "curate auction."

"I apologize for my tardiness in responding, Mrs. Pilkington. I haven't forgotten. I'm afraid I'm not yet sure of the date of my brother's wedding and I couldn't miss that."

Mrs. Pilkington's pale, reptilian eyes widened. "Would that be your brother the Earl of Sydell?"

Magnus ground his teeth; his family connections had only served to increase his appeal as a matrimonial object. "No, ma'am. It would be my eldest brother but one."

"Lord Michael?"

Melissa and the Vicar

The fact that she knew his brother's name sent a frisson of terror up his spine. Clearly she'd acquired a copy of the peerage.

The only reason she wasn't "Lord Magnusing" him all over the county was because of the vicar's comment early on in Magnus's curacy: that the title of a man of God superseded those given by men, even the King.

"Yes, it is my brother Michael who will be—" A movement across the street captured his attention. It was Miss Griffin and her unusual aunt leaving the mercantile, each carrying paper-wrapped parcels.

"Who is that?"

He turned to find Mrs. Pilkington's tiercel gaze fastened on the two women.

"That is Miss Griffin and her aunt, Mrs. Trent."

"Oh, the new tenants at Halliburton Manor."

"You know of them?" he asked in some surprise.

She gave Magnus an annoyingly smug smile. "Mr. Pilkington was instrumental in the preparation of the house."

Mr. Pilkington was in the building trade, so that was her grand way of saying her husband had done some repairs on the long-vacant cottage.

"She's come from London to partake of our healthy air," Magnus said.

Just then, Mrs. Trent threw her head back and laughed rather raucously, drawing the attention of more than one passerby.

Mrs. Pilkington frowned at this open display of revelry. "I do hope she is not a hurly-burly sort."

Her youngest daughter, Emily—the only one who didn't have a militant gleam in her eyes—squirmed at her parent's harsh statement. "*Oh, Mama.*"

Mrs. Pilkington's head whipped around, her eyes narrowing and her long nose twitching, the expression causing her to bear a striking resemblance to the ferret on the sign she had the misfortune to be standing beneath. She fixed her daughter with a freezing look. "Yes, Emily?"

The girl stared; her eyes held like a rabbit before a hawk.

Magnus stepped in. "I hope you'll excuse me, Mrs. Pilkington, but I'm afraid I'm late for Mrs. Tisdale."

An unchristian snort escaped from her mouth. "Oh, her again, is it? A creaking door hangs longest."

Minerva Spencer

Magnus suppressed the flash of irritation he felt at her unkind comment and swallowed his retort—that Mrs. Tisdale was not a creaking door, but a sick, lonely old lady. Instead he smiled, bowed, and headed off down the street. Conveniently in the same direction as Miss Griffin and her aunt, not that he had any plans to catch up with them.

The path to Mrs. Tisdale's tiny cottage pulled him off Miss Griffin's trail not far out of town, but it did not pull her out of his mind.

Magnus told himself that his interest in her was a normal reaction for any man. After all, he couldn't recall ever meeting a woman as beautiful as Miss Griffin. In addition to her striking auburn hair, creamy complexion, and remarkably voluptuous figure that her walking costume had only served to accentuate, she also possessed a kittenish upper lip that made her plush lower lip appear positively sinful. And, if all *that* wasn't enough, her tilted green eyes had sparkled with a weary humor that had shot right to his chest.

Well, to be honest, it had shot a few other places in his body, as well. Just because he was a man of the Church did not mean he was immune to beauty and feminine charms.

Magnus adjusted the strap on the battered leather satchel he always carried, the jars and bottles inside making it heavier than usual. The vicar's wife had loaded him down with calf's foot jelly and a poultice that she'd promised to one of the parishioners he planned to call on today. Magnus didn't have the heart to tell Mrs. Heeley that her jelly most often got passed from household to household until it finally ended up in a pig trough on an outlying farm.

Mrs. Heeley was widely known to be the worst cook in the county—perhaps all of Britain. But she was so good-natured that nobody wanted to hurt her feelings. And so she continued to preserve her bodyweight in dreadful jams and jellies every year, much to the chagrin of her parishioners.

"I don't know how you can bear it—all those people," Magnus's oldest brother Cecil had said the last time Magnus had gone home to visit.

Although Cecil and he were the oldest and youngest of the six brothers they were still the closest. Magnus found their mutual affection both amusing and odd because they had nothing at all in common. Cecil had no time for people—indeed, he actively avoided them—and Magnus rarely met a person he didn't like.

Melissa and the Vicar

"What *people* do you mean, Ceec?" Magnus had asked his brother.

"I mean those malingering sick people, lonely old pensioners, and desperate on-the-shelf spinsters—all clambering for your attention and clinging to you like so many limpets."

Magnus smiled now as he recalled Cecil's horror. His brother liked hunting, hounds, and horses. Other than that, Cecil seemed uninterested in the world around him, not the best characteristic for a man who would one day inherit the marquisate and its extensive properties and people.

Their parents had long despaired of him ever pulling his attention away from the sporting life long enough to marry and produce children. It wasn't that Cecil was a carouser—he didn't enjoy drinking or gambling—it was just that he had no interest in flirting, dancing, or attending house parties.

When Magnus hadn't been quick enough to refute Cecil's words his brother had continued in the same vein. "I don't understand you, Mag. You've got Briar House and a good chunk of land. With some damned fine trails," he'd added, because there was nothing more important than fox hunting. "You don't *have* to do this curate bobbery."

Magnus had been having this discussion with members of his family ever since he'd decided, at the age of fifteen, to join the clergy. By the time he was twenty he'd given up trying to explain his call to the Church. He was the first, and perhaps only, member of his family as far back as anyone knew to have shown an interest in a career usually taken— unwillingly in most instances—by second sons.

While Magnus had stopped trying to explain his calling to others, he still had to justify moving so far from home to pursue it.

"You don't need to go all the way down *South* to be a mere curate." Cecil said the word *south* as if it were a vulgar epithet. Which it was to most Yorkshiremen.

"I know that, Ceec, but I *like* New Bickford and I *like* Reverend Heeley. And, as difficult as it is for you to believe, I *like* being a curate and I *like* tending to old people, on-the-shelf spinsters, and—who else was it you said?"

Cecil had ignored his jest. "How the devil a man can engage in so much blasted praying and live like a monk, I'll never know."

The comment about living like a monk had surprised Magnus; after all, Cecil had been the most loyal man alive to his mistress, Alice Thompkins, an older widow who lived in one of the cottage on their

16

father's estate. Magnus guessed his brother would have married Mrs. Tompkins long ago if he thought his parents would permit it.

Now, Magnus's other brothers—Michael, Henry, James, and Philip—on the other hand, were a completely different story from Cecil. Tales of the earl's wild younger sons were told in every taproom in West Riding.

Lord how those four had teased Magnus when he'd turned sixteen and was still a virgin. It was a testament to his incredibly stubborn nature—which his doting mother claimed was his *only* sin—that he'd not allowed them to drag him to a brothel. But he'd stood firm. And he'd remained chaste even when other men at his seminary visited brothels or kept mistresses. Such activity wasn't encouraged, but it was tolerated as long as it was kept discrete. After all, more than one of his fellows had observed, becoming a vicar was not like becoming a Catholic priest.

No, they weren't taking a vow of celibacy, but Magnus couldn't conscience paying women to slake his physical needs. Instead, he managed his needs himself, no matter how unfulfilling that might be, and looked forward to discovering the joys of the matrimonial bed with his wife. Until that day arrived, he tried to avoid thinking too much about the sexual act if he could help it. Today, he was finding he couldn't help it.

Something about Miss Griffin had brought thoughts of a carnal nature to mind.

Magnus climbed the steps to Mrs. Tisdale's tiny house, his face burning at the images running loose in his head. It wasn't Miss Griffin's fault that she emanated a seductive sensuality that wrapped around him like the tendrils of ivy.

An unwanted surge of lust rolled through him at the thought of her tilted eyes and that long upper lip. Magnus grimaced; the innocent young woman was probably unaware of the effect her face and figure had on men.

He pushed away the lustful thoughts and rapped on the front door.

Nobody answered, so he opened it a crack and stuck his head inside. The old lady was hard of hearing and her maid-of-all-work only came in the mornings. "Mrs. Tisdale?"

There was no answer so Magnus stepped inside and lowered his satchel to the hall floor. That was when he heard a faint tapping and soft cry overhead.

Melissa and the Vicar

Magnus bolted for the narrow stairs. He'd never been anywhere on the second floor before but assumed it was where her bedchamber was.

"Mrs. Tisdale?" he called when he reached the landing, which held three doors. The first was a box room and the second a spare bedroom. He opened the third door more slowly. "Mrs. Tisdale?"

"Mister Stanwyck." The voice, breathy and hoarse, came from the far side of the bed, which was unmade but empty.

Magnus found the old lady on the hardwood floor, her leg bent at an odd angle beneath her. He dropped down beside her and gently shifted her so her weight was not on her leg. She screamed.

"I'm terribly sorry, Mrs. Tisdale," he soothed, covering her blue-veined, painfully thin legs with her flannel nightgown before turning to look at her face. Her eyes had closed and he was wondering if she'd lost consciousness when her papery lids fluttered open.

"Cold," she said, even though the house was almost unbearably warm and humid

Magnus did not think that could be good. "I'm going to lift you onto the bed where you can get warm and be more comfortable."

She grimaced but nodded.

As careful as he was picking her up, she still gave a blood curdling scream that tore at his heart. Not until he'd laid her down and covered her with the heavy quilt did he risk looking at her face.

She was staring at him, her eyes tight with pain.

"I need to go for the doctor."

Her hand shot out far faster than he'd believed she could move. "No! Not yet."

"But—"

"Just. . . don't leave me alone. Stay a moment." She was breathing too fast and bright spots of color had settled over her knife-sharp cheekbones. Her hand tightened on his, her bony fingers like the claws of a bird. "Please."

It was the first time he'd heard her speak that particular word. "Of course I'll stay." He hooked a foot around a nearby chair and pulled it toward the bed without letting go of her hand.

"Scared." Her breathing had slowed but was still jerky.

Magnus looked up from their joined hands at the word. Her blue eyes, usually so sharp and pitiless, were watery and vague.

"I'm here now, Mrs. Tisdale. Nothing to be afraid of."

18

She nodded, her gaze still fixed upon him, her grip unbreakable.

Mrs. Tisdale was the village outcast. Magnus supposed there was somebody like her in every town in Britain. He had no idea what she'd done to earn the status and he doubted her neighbors remembered, either. She'd simply occupied the role for so many decades it was like an old coat that fit too comfortably to shed.

He knew better than to ask a woman's age, but he'd seen a book she'd left open once and the flyleaf had contained the words: *"To my darling Eunice, for those times we can't be together. James"* The date below the inscription had been 1751. Even if she'd only been twenty it meant she was now somewhere in her eighties. The elegant bones of her face and her huge, deep-set eyes proclaimed she must have been a beautiful young woman.

Magnus realized her grip had loosened and her lips were parted. Her breathing was stertorous, but even and deep: she was sleeping at last.

He carefully disentangled their fingers, tip-toed from the room, and then ran with undignified haste to fetch the doctor.

***

Melissa poured herself another cup of tea—which she'd found was far easier on her stomach than coffee—and broke the seal on Joss Gormley's most recent letter. Joss wasn't only her best friend; he was also managing the brothel in Melissa's absence.

Dear Mel:

I hope this letter finds you hale, hearty, and relaxing in the village of New Bickford. Business continues as usual. Laura asks that I pass along her regards and also wanted me to remind you about the expansion she proposed just before you left on your trip.

Melissa sighed. She'd been avoiding thinking about the proposal that Laura Maitland, one of her other business partners, had made. To be honest, her heart simply hadn't been in her business since she'd coughed up blood and almost died that day last fall. A brush with mortality made one reevaluate what was important in one's life.

She frowned at the unpleasant memory of that day, took another piece of toast, and turned back to the letter.

Please don't get angry.

19

Melissa and the Vicar

Mel shook her head. "Oh, Joss. What in the world is it now?"

Laura did not stop at her reminder; she approached the owner of number nine and made an independent offer for the property, which he is currently considering.

Mel dropped her toast. "What?"

I know you wanted to wait until you, Laura, and Hugo had a chance to discuss the matter and agree on an offer for the property, but . . .

Melissa growled. She *had* wanted to wait. Now the seller, a hideously sly man, would know they wanted the building and would double the price. She ground her teeth. Laura was clearly running amok without Melissa there to curb her. While she could never love owning a brothel, The White House was her future. If she could sell it for a profit—like the woman she'd bought it from—then she could retire in the next few years. But that wouldn't happen if she paid a fortune for her next expansion.

"Bloody hell," she muttered.

I know how her behavior will have annoyed you, but it is nothing to Hugo's annoyance.

A laugh broke out of her as Joss's wry observation. "I'll wager you're correct, Joss," she said, smiling at the thought of her most prickly business partner's reaction to Laura's rash behavior.

I didn't think Hugo had it in him to feel anger—or anything other than self-love, really.

Joss despised Hugo—Melissa's most popular employee with both women and men—and made no secret of it. Of course, a lot of that dislike was due to a rather wicked trick Melissa had played on Joss a few months ago, when she'd used Hugo to get between Joss and the woman Joss had stubbornly refused to admit he loved.

It had been a foolishly dangerous plan, but it had worked.

She knew she should be grateful that the two men hadn't killed each other that night. Melissa's view was that all's well that ends well. Unfortunately, Joss hadn't seen it that way. While his anger at Melissa had abated, his loathing for Hugo had doubled. And, after he'd blackened Hugo's eye, the feeling was mutual.

Mel made a *tsking* sound at the memory and turned back to her letter.

The result of Laura's precipitate action is that Hugo and Laura hate each other more than ever. I think there will be trouble between those two before too long. I'm glad I sold my interest in the business to you. At least I don't have to worry about the two of them badgering me night and day to sell to them.

No, but Melissa would when she returned.

If I return.

Mel paused, the letter crackling between her clenched fingers. Now where had that thought come from? Of course, she was going back—where else would she go?

Her mouth tightened. Nowhere: there was nowhere else to go. At least not anywhere she wouldn't have to hide her past and who she *was*. Even staying here temporarily brought a certain amount of anxiety. Men from all over Britain knew her and there was always a possibility—nay, an *inevitability*—that she would encounter one even in a place as bucolic as New Bickford.

Well, no point dwelling on that right now. This was only her third day here and nobody had recognized her yet. The handsome curate floated into her mind. She snorted. He was one more thing she could never have and should put out of her mind. The two of them were so different they might as well be separate species.

She straightened out the crumpled sheets of paper and turned back to the letter, the rest of which was largely to do with business, some repairs, two other new employees, and a young lord whom Joss had barred from the men's side of the business for excessive debt. It wasn't until the end that he said something about himself.

My father passed quietly in his sleep last week.

She laid a hand on her throat. "Oh, Joss."

21

Melissa and the Vicar

As you know, it was a happy release. He'd become little more than a vegetable these past months and my sister was working herself to the bone.

Although she will go to Joseph, her betrothed, soon, I wish to spend a week with her before she marries. I have convinced her to take a brief holiday at the seaside. Please let me know if you would feel uncomfortable if I left Laura and Hugo in charge while I was gone for ten days.

Uncomfortable? No, that wasn't the word she'd use. *Terrified* was more like it; terrified that there might not be anything to go back to. But that was hardly Joss's fault. He'd only offered to help manage the business so that Melissa would agree to this stay in the country. He had his own life and expecting him to sacrifice it for the health of the brothel wasn't fair. Especially not when she *had* two managers who were supposed to operate the business.

She sighed and glanced down at the bottom of the page.

I miss you and hope you are well. Say hello to that spitfire Daisy from me and tell her that more than a few men are mourning her absence.

Your friend,

Joss

She folded up the letter, her mind on Joss's comment about leaving Laura and Hugo in charge: tantamount to leaving the inmates in charge of the asylum. The two whores were the worst possible combination: Laura was willful and rarely stopped to take other people into consideration.

And as for Hugo?

Just thinking his name made her head pound. Hugo was a force of nature. He was, quite frankly, the most sexually attractive man she'd ever met. It was boggling how much fascination he held for both genders— especially considering he wasn't good looking at all. His whipcord lean body, coal black eyes, and thin, cruel lips should have made him downright ugly. But there was something about him that drew and held the eye; a person would always notice Hugo in a crowded room.

He was the only employee who'd never refused a customer's request. When it came to sex, Hugo would do anything.

Leaving him in charge of her business would be putting the proverbial fox in charge of the henhouse. A fox who might ransack the building, sell all the valuables, and then set the whole thing on fire just to watch it burn.

"Melissa?"

She looked up to find Daisy standing in the doorway. "Yes?"

"Where were you? I called your name three times."

"Just thinking and relaxing—what I came here to do."

"Well, the time for relaxation is over—you've got visitors."

"At this time of day?"

"It's past noon, luv."

Mel looked at the clock on the bedside table. So it was. "Who is it?"

Daisy's full lips curved into a wicked look that had made her a lot of money over the years. "I'd hate to spoil the surprise."

Chapter Three

"Would you like another scone, Mrs. Pilkington?" Daisy had changed into a dress Mel had never seen before—a demure, high-necked pale blue gown with long sleeves. It should have made her look more "aunt-like" but it didn't.

"No, thank you, Mrs. *Trent*."

Mel hid a smile at the Pilkington woman's pointed tone and stare. She was like a bloodhound that could scent something but couldn't quite get the trail. Daisy's act wasn't fooling her for a second. They would all need to be careful around Mrs. Pilkington.

"The Summer Fête is in just three weeks," Mrs. Heeley said, blissfully unaware of any undercurrents in the room and accepting another scone, her fourth, Mel noted.

In addition to the vicar's wife there was Mrs. Pilkington and her three downtrodden daughters; Miss Agnes Philpot; her improbably named sister, Gloria; and two other women whose names Mel could not recall at the moment. An entire church committee, apparently. It seemed like an odd way to call on a complete stranger, but what did Mel know about such things?

She realized everyone was looking at her and waiting for a response. What the devil had they all been yammering about?

She looked at Daisy, who mouthed the words *summer* and *fête*.

"Ah, a fête." Mel cleared her throat. "I'm afraid I've never attended such a thing." They continued to stare. "At least not at our church in London."

Mrs. Pilkington's eyebrows shot up. "Is that so? And to what parish do you belong?"

Mel opened her mouth but couldn't make anything come out of it.

A knock on the door saved her.

Melissa and the Vicar

"Yes, Jenny?" she said, wanting to kiss the curvy young maid who appeared as guileless as a cherub but in reality, had whipped a sizeable portion of the *ton* with a riding crop.

"You've a visitor, Miss Griffin." The girl's eyes met Mel's in a way that most maids probably wouldn't and she hesitated as if she were about to deliver a wicked surprise. Melissa would have to talk to Jenny about her acting later. The girl wanted to be on the stage, so she'd better learn to embrace her role. "He says he's a *curate*." She said the word the way another person—one who hadn't worked in a brothel until a few weeks ago—might say "mermaid" or "unicorn."

"Please show him in, Jenny."

Every eye in the room swiveled toward the doorway.

"Ah, good afternoon, Miss Griffin." Reverend Stanwyck's blue eyes widened as he took in the number of people in the room. "I see I'm interrupting something—"

"You are more than welcome." Mel said a silent prayer of gratitude for the curate's distracting presence. She motioned to Daisy, "You remember my aunt, Mrs. Trent?"

"Naturally. Good afternoon, ma'am." He gave Daisy an elegant bow that brought out her carnivorous smile and Mel wanted to groan. Could the woman behave any more like a tart if she tried?

The arrival of the handsome curate threw the dynamic of the room completely off-kilter.

Mel leaned close to Daisy. "Quick, what church do I attend in London?" she whispered as the reverend bowed and greeted the cluster of women.

"Don't ask me—the only church I know of is St. Paul's."

"Good Lord. Do they even have services there?"

Daisy snorted. "Why are you asking *me* these questions?" She gestured with her chin toward the curate, who was sitting in the middle of the flock of women looking far more comfortable than any man had a right to be. "There's your local expert."

Mel gave her a filthy look.

"Two sugars and milk, please," Mister Stanwyck said to the elder Miss Philpot, who'd somehow won the competition among the women to serve him his tea when Melissa did not immediately spring to her feet.

He took the cup and saucer, thanked her, and turned to his rapt audience. "Please, I was serious about not wishing to interrupt."

2

"We were just talking about Saint Botolph's Summer Fête," Melissa said, before Mrs. Pilkington could unsheathe her claws again and reintroduce the subject of London churches.

"Yes, we were speaking of the bazaar and what we had assembled thus far." Miss Gloria Philpot was staring worshipfully at the curate and had scooted all the way to the edge of her chair, until only the tiniest sliver of rump was keeping her from falling on the floor.

"I'm not sure I understand what a bazaar *is*," Daisy said, as if she were genuinely interested.

"It is the same as a fair or market, just with a more varied selection of items rather than vegetables and such. We set up booths in the park and people sell different things. At the end of the day all the money is counted and the booth that earns the most gets a surprise gift. All the money goes toward the church windows," Mister Stanwyck said.

Ah, the church windows again. Mel really must see them.

"Mister Stanwyck has a booth where he does the loveliest portraits," one of Mrs. Pilkington's daughters piped up—the oldest, Melissa thought.

All eyes were on the man in question, who was eating his biscuit, the elegant angles of his face darkening slightly. So, this was something that embarrassed him.

Melissa couldn't resist teasing him. "Ah, you are an artist, Mr. Stanwyck."

He took a sip of tea and set down his cup and saucer before shaking his head, his lips curved in a half-smile. "No, *artist* is far too strong. I am a. . . dabbler."

The women broke into a chorus of "no's" and "you're too humble's."

But Mr. Stanwyck was determined to change the subject. "Tell me, Miss Griffin, do you have a special talent that might earn money for the windows?"

Daisy choked and spewed tea into her lap. Mr. Stanwyck was immediately on his feet, hovering over her with an expression of concern on his beautiful face. "I say, are you quite alright, Mrs. Trent?"

Mel leaned close to Daisy and smacked her on the back. Hard.

"I'm fine," Daisy wheezed, lurching to her feet. "Please, excuse me." She clamped both hands over her mouth and fled the room. Mel imagined her collapsing with laughter in the kitchen and entertaining the others with the curate's innocent question.

Melissa and the Vicar

"Would you like to go after her and—" Mr. Stanwyck began, his brow furrowed with concern. "Help her?" he finished lamely.

Mel gave him a grim smile. "I daresay she'll be fine. Tell me," she said, adopting a softer tone, "what do some of the other booths sell?"

"Mrs. Heeley sells some of the jams and jellies she makes during the year." A pregnant silence followed this declaration.

"One year Farmer Sinclair brought ice and we had raspberry ices—in the middle of *summer!*" This was Emily Pilkington, the youngest of the three girls and by far the least like her mother.

"My sister and I sell wool stockings." This from one of the women whose name Mel didn't know.

Mrs. Pilkington made a derisive sound. "My daughters and I will be selling various needlework projects, such as antimacassars." Her expression was virtuous—as if God preferred chair covers to wool stockings.

"Lady Barclay donates cut flowers from her hot-houses," Miss Philpot added, not to be outdone by Mrs. Pilkington, a woman she clearly viewed as her nemesis.

Mel wondered where Lady Barclay was today and why she hadn't converged on her with all the others.

"Sir Thomas and Lady Barclay have not yet returned from London," Mrs. Heeley said, as if Mel had spoken out loud.

"They go every year for the Season." Mrs. Pilkington bristled with pride, basking in the reflected glow of her august neighbors.

"Last year Agnes and I sold potted herbs." This from Miss Gloria Philpot, whose pronouncement earned her a repressive look from Mrs. Pilkington. A tense silence settled over the room.

Mr. Stanwyck cleared his throat. "Ah, distribution from each unto every man according to his—or her—need, as it were," the curate interjected when the two formidable women engaged in a staring match.

Miss Philpot and Mrs. Pilkington turned to Mr. Stanwyck but Mel couldn't help noticing that neither woman looked entirely convinced by his aphorism.

"Is that from the Bible?" Mel asked, amused by his attempts to restore peace.

Once again, she caught a glimpse of unholy humor in his heavenly blue eyes. "Yes—from Acts."

Mrs. Heeley gave the young curate a possessive, motherly smile. "The vicar always says he's never had a curate with such extensive knowledge of scripture as Mr. Stanwyck."

The other women clucked with approval—even the two combatants settled their feathers—while the man in question squirmed.

"How very commendable, Mr. Stanwyck." Mel had to bite her lip to keep from laughing when he gave her a narrow-eyed look.

The rest of the visit passed quickly, with each of the women vying to out-extoll the curate's virtues.

Daisy resurfaced just as the visitors were taking their leave, dexterously thwarting Mrs. Pilkington's efforts to time her departure with the curate's.

As a result, Mel and Mr. Stanwyck were the last two in the entry hall while Daisy strong-armed the Pilkington brood into the back garden under the laughable pretext of needing advice about local flora. The closest Daisy ever came to nature was the silk flowers in her monstrous hats.

Mr. Stanwyck held his hat in his hands as he looked down at her, smiling. "You were wicked to have challenged my biblical knowledge while I attempted to smooth the waters earlier, Miss Griffin."

"Oh? I don't know what you mean, sir." Mel knew she could do innocence as well as a vestal virgin—whatever those might be. Perhaps it was in the Old Testament and Mr. Stanwyck might spend some time instructing her . . .

"You don't fool me for an instant."

Mel chuckled. "I'm sorry, that *was* wicked of me. But you have to admit you deserved it. All that petting and stroking can't be good for you—you'll end up with an insufferably big head. Look what so much praise has done to Hector?"

"Did you just compare me to a rooster, Miss Griffin?"

"I would never do such a thing. But if I *had*, I would've thought you'd treasure such a comparison given Hector's *titan* status in the community."

"Touché." He gave her a smile that did something odd to her chest. Melissa was trying to figure out exactly what it was when he asked, "By the by, you did an excellent job of dodging the question of what you might do at our fête."

5

Melissa and the Vicar

"Are you calling me dodgy, Mr. Stanwyck?" she asked, her tone a perfect echo of his.

"I would never say such a thing," he mocked, not to be outdone.

Mel laughed.

He clapped his hat on his head and bowed. "I'm afraid I must be getting on, Miss Griffin. Please give my regards to your aunt and tell her I'm sorry I could not wait to say goodbye." He paused at the bottom of the steps and smiled. "You've got less than three weeks to come up with something for the fête."

Mel admired his tall, broad-shouldered physique as he strode down the walk, suddenly wishing he would stop, come back, and . . . *what?*

Just as he reached the end of the walk she called out. "What happens if I don't come up with anything? Will I end up in the public stocks?"

Rich laughter filled the emptiness between them. "Nothing quite like the prospect of a public shaming to motivate a person!" he called over his shoulder.

And then he disappeared around the hedge.

***

Although Magnus couldn't have said *why*, he was more than a little surprised when Sunday arrived and Miss Griffin and her aunt appeared in church. She'd not said she was *not* coming, but neither had she appeared enthusiastic when the vicar had mentioned it.

They arrived a few moments late and took seats in the very back pew, the one closest to the door, as if they were already planning for their escape.

It was not his week to deliver the sermon, a fact for which he found himself inexplicably grateful. He'd never felt shy about speaking in church before. In fact, he enjoyed both contemplating and drafting his sermons. So why was he grateful he wasn't delivering one today? Was it because he could imagine the mocking expression she'd wear while listening to any sermon of his?

And just why did he imagine she would look that way? She'd given no indication of . . . well, of *impiety*. So why would he think such a thing?

The truth was that she'd done nothing to engender such suspicions. No, it was more the way she looked. Magnus felt ashamed just thinking such a horrid thought—as if the way his body responded to her beauty was somehow evidence of *her* wicked nature, rather than his own lustful imaginings.

Minerva Spencer

He gave a slight shake of his head; his thoughts when it came to Miss Griffin were very Old Testament in nature and he should devote serious consideration as to why he viewed her in such a light.

It also bothered Magnus more than he liked to admit that the thought of potential mockery from her—or from *anyone*, for that matter—would discountenance him when it came to his faith or his calling. Yes, he would get to the heart of the matter when he next meditated.

But for now, he tried to concentrate on worthier matters—like Mrs. Tisdale. He liked the cantankerous old woman and knew that being bedbound with a broken leg would likely drive her—and Dori, the poor girl he'd engaged to look after her—to distraction. Even though he knew Mrs. Tisdale would be in a *mood*, he was still looking forward to visiting her after church today.

Mr. Heeley gave a sermon on turning the other cheek, a barely veiled reference to Mr. Dawkins and his neighbors, the Misses Philpot, who'd resumed the same battle they fought every year: Mr. Dawkins's garden versus the sisters' ever-increasing flock, led by their beloved Hector.

Magnus's gaze wandered along with his attention, settling in the same place no matter how many times he wrenched it away. Miss Griffin had been here barely a week and already he believed she appeared healthier. She was still fragile-looking and lovely, but no longer as pale.

She looked up and caught him staring.

His chest froze even though the rest of him burned. He wanted to look away; indeed, it was the polite thing to do. But he couldn't. She held him captive, her green eyes as shrouded in secrets as a medieval forest. In that instant, Magnus felt sure that she saw the images his fertile imagination created when he was alone in his tiny curate's cottage at night. In his bed.

The corners of her mesmerizing lips turned up so slightly he wasn't sure he hadn't imagined it. And then she looked away.

It was as if a large fist released him and he snorted air through his nose, just like a drowning man gasping for air.

***

Getting Daisy out of bed, in a respectable dress, and on the footpath toward the church had taken every bit of energy Melissa possessed.

"I though you came out all the way to the back of beyond to rest and sleep and get better," the older woman groused, her carefully cultivated accent dropping away in her anger. "If I'd known you'd planned on

7

gettin' up before the cock's crow and gettin' all churchy on me I never would have come."

They'd been passing the Philpot cottage at the time and Daisy had lowered her voice to a hiss, neither of them interested in catching Hector's attention.

"I'm paying you to behave like a respectable guardian," Mel reminded her after they'd scurried past unscathed. "Why else did you think I wanted you here? For a quick frig and a ride on that dirty mouth of yours?"

Daisy muttered something under her breath.

Mel stopped and grabbed her arm, pulling her to a halt. "What did you say?"

Daisy yanked herself away. "I *said* maybe that is exactly what you need. When's the last time you've had anyone between your legs, man *or* woman? If you ask me, what you really need is a proper fuck to sort you out and get you out o' this black mood you been in for months."

"Well, I *didn't* ask you."

Daisy crossed her arms. "No, you didn't. You don't ask nobody nothin'—you're too much smarter, than the rest of us, aren't you? But let me tell *you* somethin', Madam Melissa Bloody Griffin, you ain't fooling me. You're miserable and heartsick and no amount o' church or dressin' prissy or movin' to the country will help you get away from yerself."

Melissa worked her jaw from side to side, willing herself to calm down. She refused to do this—to argue with an employee. Because that's what Daisy was: her employee. They'd been friends and equals once, long ago, but that changed the day Melissa purchased the brothel. Now, Melissa employed eighty-one people; that was *eighty-one* livelihoods she held in her hands—eighty-one futures that relied on her making the right decisions.

And all the while she was making sure people got fed, paid, and housed, there were *other* people—men, mostly—who'd like nothing better than to take away what was hers. And there were other men—*moral* men—who just wanted to shut her business down. And then there were those in authority who wanted a piece of the pie to keep their mouths shut. And then there were her own qualms that woke her in the middle of the night—yes, in her *empty* bed—about making her money off the backs of others.

The old arguments she'd always used—that at least she gave whores a safer, healthier, and more prosperous place to do the job they did—well, those arguments were as frayed around the edges as a ragged blanket that no longer offered comfort.

But, at the end of the day, all of that was just so much philosophical dithering that she couldn't afford. A woman like her had two options: either being alone at the top or being used and abused at the bottom. Melissa knew she would take the first of those options every single time.

She looked up at Daisy, who stood a good five inches taller than her. "If you don't want to play the part I'm paying you to play then say so and you can go back to London and I'll send for some other *aunt*. And don't think I haven't noticed you twistin' Jenny and Sarah's tails and makin' them behave badly, too." Jenny and Sarah were two of the younger whores Mel had brought along to act as domestics in this farce. They were good girls, but this was the first time they'd been out of London and they were both eagerly, and easily, led into mischief. "I know it's been you encouragin' them to sneak out at night, Daisy."

Just like Daisy, Mel let her own St. Giles accent slip into her words when she became excited or annoyed; all those years of careful practice gone in a heartbeat.

Mel shook her head in disgust; Christ, give her anything but a whiney whore first thing in the morning.

"You do what you want, Daisy. I'm going to church." Mel set off without looking back. Only when she heard a scuffing sound behind her did she know Daisy had followed.

They trudged for a while in silence, Mel slowing a bit, until they were walking side by side again.

Daisy was the first to speak, just as they'd both known she would be. It wasn't because Mel employed her; no, Daisy spoke first because Mel's ability to carry a grudge was legendary. It wasn't something she was proud of, but she had to admit that she'd die of thirst rather than open her mouth to ask for a glass of water if she was angry enough.

"I'm sorry for getting the other girls riled up."

Mel grunted.

"And I'm sorry about the way I've been riding you. I'll do better about being . . . aunt-ish."

"Good."

9

Melissa and the Vicar

After that Daisy filled the walk with chatter, knowing better than to expect too much in response. Another thing Mel wasn't proud of was how long it took her to shift her mood back once she'd gotten angry. But by the time they arrived at the small church—late, by the look of it—she'd calmed down enough to ask Daisy how she looked.

Daisy tweaked a hair into place, adjusted her hat a fraction, and smiled. "You look bloomin'."

Mel smiled up at her. "So do you."

And then Melissa entered a church for the first time in her life.

***

Ten minutes felt like ten hours. The bench was hard and unforgiving, Reverend Heeley's voice droned on and on, his sermon was achingly boring, and the other parishioners far too interested in Melissa for her comfort. In fact, the only good thing about the entire ordeal was Mister Stanwyck sitting right up front like a prized ornament on a mantelpiece. Her brain hadn't exaggerated his handsome, angelic looks; he *deserved* to be sitting up front and visible.

Mel entertained herself by wondering what he was thinking. His handsome features were fixed in an expression of thoughtful attentiveness, as if every word that fell from the vicar's lips—and there were a lot of them—was of the utmost importance.

But his eyes betrayed him. They found Mel again and again and again.

At first, she pretended she didn't feel the weight of his stare. But just once, she let their eyes meet and lock. Daisy had finally needed to nudge her in the ribs.

"Oye," she hissed. "You've stop breathing."

She had. But so had he—she'd seen it on his face. She'd also heard him suck in air from all the way in the back of the church.

He avoided meeting her gaze again and the rest of the service was a misery.

When it seemed like things might be over Daisy whispered, "Are we staying to do the pretty? Or do you want to leave now?"

Mel wanted to see him—to talk to him—but she knew what it would be like once the doors opened: a cloud of females as thick as summer flies would descend on him.

So, they'd left early, drawing several scandalized looks from those in the immediate vicinity. Well, that was too bad.

"I'm going home and crawling back into bed," Daisy said with a huge yawn as they let themselves out the back lychgate.

Mel was too edgy to rest, and if she went home, she'd just fret about what was going on in London, what Hugo and Laura were up to, and a hundred other things that she'd promised herself she'd leave behind.

She reminded herself that she'd made the effort to come all this way to get healthy; she might as well give it a fair try.

What had Joss said to her when he'd seen her off that last day? "Go for long walks, Mel. Even if you don't think you want to, you'll be glad you did."

So Mel said, "I'm going for a walk."

Daisy stared. "Walking back home *is* a walk."

Mel ignored her and turned toward town. If she recalled correctly, there had been other paths; maybe one of them led down to the water. New Bickford wasn't directly on the water but she knew it wasn't too far off. She'd been here almost a week and still not dipped her toes in the ocean—another thing Joss had suggested. Mel should have asked somebody the best way to get to the water—some of the surrounding cliffs were far too steep to use—but one had to get to water if one just kept walking, didn't one?

She followed the path, taking the first left she came to. Almost immediately she found herself in a surprisingly dense stand of trees. Mel hesitated, wondering if she'd wandered onto somebody's private footpath.

Well, if they wanted her off it, they could tell her so.

The wooded area ended abruptly and she came out of the trees into a little clearing. Not far ahead the path ran beside a cottage. Mel paused and looked around. There were no out buildings, no garden to speak of, nothing, just a little house that looked to have sprung from the ground itself. Yet it appeared well-tended, so somebody must live in it.

Mel was about to resume her journey when the front door flew open and a whirlwind in skirts came flying out.

"You—you *evil* old witch!" the whirlwind yelled into the house, which looked dark beyond the doorway.

Faint laughter drifted from inside the house. The girl slammed the door—which sprang back open and hit the wall instead of closing—and spun around, shrieking when she saw Melissa.

Melissa and the Vicar

Mel raised her hands in a gesture meant to be calming, but the woman flinched away.

"Are you here for *her*?" she demanded. But then she turned and spat on the ground, not waiting for an answer. "If you know what's good for you, you'll leave without stepping foot into her web." And with that she stormed past close enough that her skirts brushed against Mel's.

The little clearing was once again quiet, the only sound that of the door as it softly tapped against the wall.

What had all *that* been about?

Mel squinted through the doorway into the house; she could see nothing.

Tap, tap, tap.

Mel yelped and spun around. What in the—

Tap, tap, tap.

The noise came from overhead and she looked up to find an old woman peering down from a closed window. She pointed at Mel and made a beckoning motion: come in.

Mel stared and the woman beckoned again.

She dropped her eyes to the doorway the deranged woman had just stormed out of, a picture forming in her mind. The woman upstairs was obviously bedridden and the girl who'd stormed off had been her caretaker. She chewed her lip, wondering what kind of woman could make another woman *that* angry.

Tap, tap, tap.

Well, it seemed like she was about to find out.

She sighed, picked up her skirts, and climbed the steps.

More books by S.M. LaViolette, Minerva Spencer, & S.M. Goodwin:

THE ACADEMY OF LOVE SERIES

THE MUSIC OF LOVE
A FIGURE OF LOVE
A PORTRAIT OF LOVE*
THE LANGUAGE OF LOVE*

THE OUTCASTS SERIES

DANGEROUS
BARBAROUS
SCANDALOUS

THE REBELS OF THE *TON*

NOTORIOUS*
OUTRAGEOUS*
INFAMOUS*

THE MASQUERADERS SERIES

THE FOOTMAN
THE POSTILION*
THE BASTARD*

THE SEDUCERS SERIES:

MELISSA AND THE VICAR
JOSS AND THE COUNTESS
HUGO AND THE MAIDEN*

S.M.'s Historical Erotic Romance Series:
VICTORIAN DECADENCE

HIS HARLOT*
HIS VALET*
HIS COUNTESS*

<u>ANTHOLOGIES:</u>

<u>BACHELORS OF BOND STREET</u>
<u>THE ARRANGEMENT</u>

<u>S.M. Goodwin's Historical Mystery</u>
<u>LIGHTNER & LAW Series:</u>

ABSENCE OF MERCY*

*Forthcoming

About the Author

Minerva Spencer has been a criminal prosecutor, college history teacher, B&B operator, dock worker, ice cream manufacturer, reader for the blind, motel maid, and bounty hunter.

Okay, so the part about being a bounty hunter is a lie.

Minerva does, however, know how to hypnotize a Dungeness crab, sew her own Regency Era clothing, knit a frog hat, juggle, rebuild a 1959 American Rambler, and gain control of Asia (and hold on to it) in the game of RISK.

Minerva Spencer also writes historical romance and historical erotic romance under the name S.M. LaViolette, and historical mystery under the name S.M. Goodwin

CPSIA information can be obtained
at www.ICGtesting.com
Printed in the USA
LVHW010325210322
713970LV00005B/416

9 781951 662240